N

L

—

—

—|

—

—

—↓

—

—

—

|-

—

B₄

—

—

—

—

M
tic]

Dead Man's Guns

The killer Frank Lavender was dead, so how could it be that he was involved in a gunfight at Hoyt's Camp, a logging town along Wyoming's Snake River? Either Lavender had found a way to cheat Death or it was someone else using the gunman's name.

Lyle Colbert didn't like it either way for Frank Lavender, or whoever it was, had come to town to destroy Lyle Colbert, supposedly out of love for the pretty Tess Bright.

It wasn't certain if Tess reciprocated the gunman's love, but it did not matter for she would have no time to make up her mind. Colbert was determined to kill Frank Lavender. Again.

Dead Man's Guns

Logan Winters

A Black Horse Western

ROBERT HALE · LONDON

© Logan Winters 2010
First published in Great Britain 2010

ISBN 978-0-7090-8843-1

Robert Hale Limited
Clerkenwell House
Clerkenwell Green
London EC1R 0HT

www.halebooks.com

Typeset by
Derek Doyle & Associates, Shaw Heath
Printed and bound in Great Britain by
CPI Antony Rowe, Chippenham and Eastbourne

ONE

His horse was down, shot out from under him and so he had no choice but to run on afoot. The five men behind him would catch up soon, but the broken ground would keep them from being able to race their ponies after him. Soon, though, they would break from the pine forest and shoot him down like a dog if he slowed his pace.

His own boots slipped out from under him as he ran across the rocky earth. Twice he fell, once losing his grip on his Colt revolver. Scrambling, he managed to retrieve it, although the three loads left in its cylinder would not be enough to deter his pursuers. They wanted him dead.

The running man's hair was in his eyes, his face streaked with sweat and dirt. He could hear their horses now, and glancing back he saw the first hunting man, riding a pinto pony, rifle in his hands, emerge from the verge of the forest. The running man's chest was burning, his legs were heavy as lead. He looked desperately for shelter, but saw none, no place to hide to make his last stand.

He drew up abruptly, a desolate curse rising from his throat. He had run himself out of luck. He knew now where he was, and there was no possible escape.

He stood on the rim-rock of the Snake River Gorge looking down at the raging river a hundred feet below him, the tumbling water frothing and surging as it roared its westward way out of the Yellowstone country toward the Columbia River. The water was roiling, angry and proud in its strength.

A shot rang out from behind him and then a second which tore through his shoulder, turning him half around with its violent impact. Five horsemen now appeared from the dark line of pine trees, all of them with guns blazing. The running man turned and leapt into space, rolling and tumbling toward the river below. Inside his skull, he felt the shock of an impact far greater than that of the searcher's rifle bullet and realized that he had hit his head against solid stone. He had a brief, confused glimpse of the sheer cliff, the surging white waters of the chill Snake River, the thin veil of high August clouds above, and then as he sank into the cold waters of the river and the rapids thundered around him, he remembered no more.

When Teresa Bright had filled the water buckets, she paused for a while to rinse her face and wash her feet in the cold, clear water of the river. Here where the gorge widened and the waters spread, calming themselves after their furious rush through the canyon, the current was swift, but no longer dangerous. Scattered light fell through the willow trees at the water's edge, scattering gold coins along the dark bank. A loon cried somewhere and frogs groused along the river's edge. She had removed her boots and eased nearer to the bank at her accustomed spot when she saw *it* bobbing against the shore among the cattails.

She did not scream or cry out but she backed swiftly away. She was a western woman, and she had seen much of violence. Still, the small blond girl was terrified. The man wore a red shirt and black jeans, both of which were badly torn. He was unmoving, beached on a sandbar a few yards from the riverbank.

She was sure that he was dead, since no one in memory, Indian or white, had ever navigated the Snake River rapids and lived.

She crept nearer to him, moving cautiously along the muddy bank of the river. Peering at him, she saw a man in his twenties, his face lean and sun-burned, a stripe of new scar across his jaw. His dark hair, now matted with mud and the blood of a recent injury, curled at the back of his neck. His broad hands looked strong and capable, and as Teresa studied them one of the dead man's fingers twitched.

Teresa's hands went to her mouth and she backed away, her eyes wider yet. The man's arm moved. Only slightly, but enough to demonstrate that there was life lingering in the motionless body. Gathering her skirts again, barefoot still, Teresa turned and ran, leaving her water pails behind.

The cabin was made of unbarked logs and rested on a low rocky rise among the dark pines. Teresa reached it, leaped up the swayed steps and banged open the plank door.

'Well, there you are at last,' the tiny old woman standing at the primitive rock and steel plate stove said. 'And where's the water you were sent for?'

'Where's Pa?' Teresa asked, unable to catch her breath.

'What is it?' the old woman demanded. She stood with a wooden spoon in her hand staring at the girl, her pinched features hardened with displeasure.

'I found a man along the river,' Teresa managed to say. 'Either dead or dying. I need Pa or Andy to go back with me.'

'Look around to the woodpile,' the old lady said without much concern or show of interest. She returned to her cooking, stirring the quietly burbling contents of a black iron pot.

Teresa left the house at a run, leapt from the porch and rounded the cabin corner to the woodpile. There, a lanky man wearing a faded red long-john shirt and twill trousers held up with suspenders was positioning a length of cordwood he intended to split with his axe. The day was cool, but he was perspiring. Now he lowered his axe and mopped his forehead with an old bandana as his daughter appeared. He frowned at her expression. He asked first: 'Indians?' his voice weary and anguished at once. They had faced too many Indian raids in their ten-year stand along the river.

'No, Pa,' Teresa said. She took her father's hand and tugged at him, all the while reporting what she had discovered along the river. Placing the axe carefully aside, her father picked up his battered flop hat, secured it on his head and collected his old army-issue .45-70 Springfield rifle.

Orson Bright was frowning heavily as he accompanied his daughter through the deep shade of the wind-swayed pines, hearing the constant rush of the big river beyond the tight ranks of the trees. They did not need more trouble around here. Not just now.

The trouble with Santana was barely over, costing Bright one of his two grown sons and now this Colbert bunch was prowling the timberlands. Approaching sixty years of age, Orson figured he had earned the right to live out his life in peace. It looked like it wasn't to be.

Tess – Teresa – slowed her eager pace as they approached the river's edge. Here the sunlight which revealed itself as slanting beams through the tall trees became brilliant, glinting off the long-flowing river. Tess halted and lifted a pointing finger. Orson nodded, gripping his rifle more tightly. Among the clotted cattails on the sandbar was a man, his boots dragging in the river current. Alive or dead, he could not tell, but Orson Bright disliked it either way. He took a deep breath and started forward, his face set grimly.

The river flowed on in its ceaseless way, its silver-blue face constantly changing. Orson gestured to Teresa to hold back, then he crossed the shallow inlet to where the man's body lay.

Crouching down, Orson lifted the motionless man's wrist and felt for a pulse. It was there, faint but steady. Orson rose heavily. One more problem to be dealt with. It would have been easier with a corpse. Dig a shallow grave and, after a few words from the Good Book, walk away.

Teresa watched from the riverbank, the breeze shifting her blond hair, her hands clasped together. Orson nodded to her.

'He's alive. Get your boots on and get on back to the house. He's too big for me to shoulder. If Andy hasn't come home yet, bring the mule to help us.' After a pause, Orson told Tess, who was busy tying her bootlaces, 'Best take the water pails along with you. Mother Rose will be peeved if you forget them a second time.'

Some of the water came in handy very soon. Mother Rose – Orson's deceased wife's mother – had a potful of it boiling away furiously on the stove as she cut the injured man's red shirt away with a pair of sewing scissors. Laying the stranger down on a cot in what had been Orson's other son's, Dan's, room before the gunman, Santana, had killed him, they quickly discovered the darker red stain on the faded shirt just below the collarbone.

'Bullet wound,' Orson had pronounced.

Mother Rose, whose pinched appearance gave a first impression of an uncaring crone, was only an old woman who had struggled long in the harsh West, losing her daughter and grandson to the land. Her habitual expression was a reflection of the unkind world, concealing a warm heart. She worked now with skilled, amazingly gentle fingers at the savage wound in the stranger's shoulder. Tess watched uncertainly from the doorway. Her father, in what might have seemed callous to a casual observer, had gone back outside to continue chopping firewood. It was simply that he could do nothing to help Rose, and his chore was a necessary one if they were to have heat and warm food.

'Who do you think he could be?' Teresa asked Mother Rose, expecting no answer. 'An outlaw, do you suppose?'

'Help me roll him over, Tess,' Rose said. 'I need to see if the bullet's passed through or if I have to go to carving.'

The choice of words sent a little shudder through Tess, but she went to the bedside of the dying man, and the women working together, managed to get him rolled onto his stomach. Not once did the badly injured man make a sound.

'Well, I'll be,' Rose said. 'Do you see that little pucker on his back here, Tess? That's the bullet, sure as blazes. That tells me he was shot from a distance, else it would have passed all the way through.'

'What do you have to do?' Teresa asked.

'Get me my six-inch knife,' Rose said. Tess looked uncertain, vaguely frightened. A smile actually creased Rose's pinched face. 'This is nothing, girl. No more than lancing a boil, which

13

I've done many a time. Get the knife, scoot, and then I'll need you to hold the lantern right over where I'm working.'

True to Rose's prediction, the slug slid out past the incision easily. There was a flow of crimson blood, but nothing like Tess had expected and feared. They cleaned up the wounds, entrance and exit, as well as they could with lye soap and carbolic acid, and tightly wrapped a bandage of clean linen around the stranger's chest. Orson had returned and stood observing their handiwork.

'Well?' he asked.

'I don't know,' Rose said rising. 'It doesn't seem the bullet broke a bone, but he's in deep shock. Like when Paddy got kicked by that mule.'

'What do you mean?'

'Step over here,' the old woman said. 'On the back of his skull there's a lump the size of a goose egg. Whatever caused that might have done more damage than the rifle bullet. Could be his skull is cracked open. Could be he won't make it no matter what we do.' Rose was wiping her hands on her apron. She looked away from her patient and started toward the kitchen. 'Anyway, I got to fix supper now – somebody's got to do it.'

14

Orson went out as well, to wash up for supper. Teresa lingered for another minute, watching the young man who slept so deeply that it seemed he might never rise again. Mother Rose didn't think he would make it. Teresa wanted him to, wanted very much for the handsome young man to survive. She could have not explained her feelings; there was no explanation.

She only knew that she badly wanted the stranger to pull through somehow. She turned the lantern down low and went out to help with serving supper. Outside, soft rain had begun to fall across the pine forest.

'What are you going to do with him?' Andy Bright demanded around a mouthful of cornbread and beef stew. Tess looked across the table at her brother who now, in his late teens, had filled out across the chest and shoulders with solid muscle. His bullish neck supported a broad, manly face shaded with dark beard stubble. 'He sure can't stay here,' Andy continued. 'We don't even know who he is. Besides, from what you're telling me he might never get well. Isn't that right?'

'We can't throw him back in the river, like a caught fish we decided we didn't want,' Orson

Bright said reasonably.

'I don't see why not!' Andy said. Tess did not know if her brother was joking or not. It was hard to tell with Andy. 'Did anybody go through his pockets?'

'We did,' Orson answered. 'There was nothing there to tell us who he is.'

'You two better think twice about anything you decide.' Mother Rose said. She had her face bent toward her bowl of stew. Strands of gray-streaked hair had slipped free of their pins, augmenting her crone-like appearance. Andy glared at the old woman. To his mind, foolish old people, like children, should be seen and not heard.

'What do you mean, Mother?' Orson inquired. He had dunked a slab of cornbread into his stew and now sat holding it halfway to his lips, the gravy dripping onto the rough plank table top.

'Just what I said,' Rose answered, still not looking up as she continued to spoon the stew from her bowl. 'You better think twice.' The old woman lifted her head now and dabbed at her lips with the corner of her apron.

Fixing her bright eyes on Orson, she said, 'You two didn't find anything on the man, in his pockets to identify who he was, did you? You

16

should have looked closer.'

'What do you mean? Did he have some papers on him? Something like that?' Andy asked.

'Not exactly,' the old woman said. 'Tess – get me the wounded man's shirt!'

Teresa placed her napkin aside, rose and went to the room where the injured man lay. Orson and Andy watched Rose's face, seeing a small light of triumph in the old woman's eyes. Tess was back within a minute. She had spared a moment to touch the wounded young man's feverish forehead before snatching up his blood-stained red shirt and returning with it to the dining room. She handed the folded garment to her grandmother.

Rose unfolded the torn shirt as Orson rose to go closer to her. Andy, his coffee cup in hand, watched with glowering attention.

Rose found what she wanted and offered the shirt to Orson's inspection. Her gnarled finger tapped at two tiny objects on the upper left breast of the shirt. Orson's forehead furrowed slightly as he saw what she was indicating.

'What is it, Dad?' Andy demanded.

'You know what those are?' Rose asked, looking up to Orson.

'I do, yes,' he answered.

Andy could restrain himself no longer. The young man rose abruptly, his heavy chair scraping against the wooden floor. Throwing his napkin aside he rounded the table toward his father and grandmother.

'What is it?' Andy demanded again. With his habitual impatience he snatched the shirt away and examined it. 'I don't see anything,' he said, tossing the shirt back on the table.

With more forbearance than the young hothead deserved, Mother Rose turned the shirt over once more and pointed to the two small metal inserts in the fabric. 'Do you know what these are?' she asked. Andy only shrugged.

'Grommets,' Orson Bright told his son, fingering the small brass eyelets set two vertical inches apart.

'So?' Andy asked, growing flushed with anger as he often did when he failed to comprehend matters.

'No earthly use at all on the front of a man's shirt,' Orson told him. 'Except one – they would keep the fabric from being damaged . . . if the man wore a badge.'

TWO

Dawn light awakened him and brought the return of pain. A dull thumping ache in his skull, a lancet of fiery pain in his shoulder. He tried to move that arm, but found it bound tightly and so he had to jackknife himself into a sitting position. With his hair hanging in his eyes he stared sullenly at the rectangle of light the rising sun cast against the wooden floor. There was a picture of an eagle in flight hung on the white-washed wall. The bed was of puncheon, roughly hewn, the quilt of patchwork design draping his lap and legs. Well and good.

But where was he?

That jarring question brought an even more puzzling enquiry to the surface of his foggy thoughts:

Who was he?

He had no idea if he was a tradesman, mule-skinner, farmer or thief. No name suggested itself – a man's most personal possession. His name, his mark of pride, and sometimes of shame . . . was that it? Was he a criminal on the run?

The wound in his shoulder suggested a bullet wound, so that was a possibility. Maybe he had been on some ill-considered outlaw raid, been shot and managed to drag himself back to the gang's hideout. Or perhaps he was a hostage. Or a farmer who had suffered a hunting accident and was now recovering in the bosom of his caring family. Perhaps none of these.

His head ached as he considered the innumerable possibilities. He was unformed, a creature of mud waiting to be modeled into something human, something with a past, a future. He couldn't have been more depressed if he had awakened to find himself standing on a gallows.

The door swung open slowly. The girl entered hesitantly, a tray covered with a muslin cloth supported by one slender arm. Her smile was an uncomfortable one. She placed the tray down, parted the curtains on the window and spoke her few words without ever really looking into his eyes.

'Biscuits and honey. I'll fetch coffee.'

And then she was gone, the lingering scent of youth and lye soap in the air, her presence unexplained. Was she someone he knew? A sister, a relative – a wife! His lover whom he did not even recognize, to whom he had not responded as expected.

He rubbed his forehead with the heel of his hand, stretched out his fingers for a buttered biscuit and chewed on it dourly, staring at the door which the young woman had left ajar.

She returned, a quart-sized blue coffee pot in her hands. She glanced at the tray on the bedside table and smiled.

'You don't care for honey?'

He didn't know. Did he? He had been too urgently hungry to spoon it from the pot. Probably he cared for honey. He started to swing his legs to the side of his bed, became aware of his nakedness beneath the bed clothes and sat up carefully. The girl was at the window, her eyes on the sun-bright pine forest beyond the glass.

'I don't seem to be able to recall your name,' he said dully.

21

'No, you wouldn't,' she said brightly, turning to face him. 'I'm Tess. Do you remember meeting me along the river?'

'No.' He rubbed his head again, nearly slapping at it as if that would jar some memory free. 'I have to ask . . . do you know me? Can you tell me who I am?'

'You still don't know?' she said, approaching the bed with concern in her eyes. 'We . . . I . . . thought that a night's rest might bring your memory back.'

'It hasn't, I'm afraid,' he answered grimly. 'Can't you tell me?'

'No,' she said too hastily. There seemed to be a hint of fear in her eyes. She touched her throat uneasily with slender fingertips. She had been warned to tell him nothing. To make no guesses as to his identity. Father had said, correctly, 'We don't really know who this man is. Conjecture will solve nothing. When he's back on his feet, we'll turn him out. That's all there is to it The rest is his problem, not ours.'

'I . . .' he said uneasily, spooning honey onto another biscuit, 'am no one you know, no one from around here? Where am I, anyway!' he asked with a surge of confusion.

'It's called the Tumano Basin. Right near the Snake River. Teton country.'

He shook his head. It was filled with the buzzing of confused bees. 'I don't know—'

'Wyoming!' the girl, Tess said with some frustration.

'Wyoming,' the wounded man said in a sort of mingled wonder and acceptance. After pondering that for a moment, he asked, 'There was nothing . . . Tess . . . in my pockets, my saddlebags, to indicate who I was?'

'You had no horse,' she said. 'There was nothing in your pockets.'

'Nothing? Isn't that strange?' he asked, frowning.

'I don't know. Who among us has anything worth carrying?'

'We're not. . . ? You and I . . . are we alone here?' he asked.

'No! Certainly not. My family lives in this house. It is our home.'

'And I am a stranger?'

'You are a stranger,' Tess said. She was hurriedly collecting the coffee pot and the tray from the bedside table. He continued to hold the coffee cup between both hands, studying the way she moved, the firm lines of her throat and jaw, the quick darting of her blue eyes, the glint of morning sunlight in her golden hair.

'Tess?' he asked as she turned to go. She did not face him.

'Yes?'

'Will you do something for me? Will you christen me?'

'Will I—' she choked on her laughter. 'Whyever?'

'I wish to have a name to go by, Tess. Even a dog is given a name to respond to.'

'As you wish,' she said after a moment. Considering for a long minute, her features pinched with concentration, she finally offered: 'Ned.'

'Ned?'

'It's as good a name as any other,' Tess replied. 'It just popped into my head. You look like a Ned.'

'Do I?'

'If you don't like it, choose your own!' Tess said, flushing for no apparent reason.

'Ned is fine. Is it short for anything?'

'No, it's just . . . Ned.'

'And a last name?'

24

'Do you need one of those?' Tess asked as if tiring of the game. 'All right . . . keep it simple, shall we. Browning. Ned Browning – unless you object,' she said with a bit of irritation.

'It's a fine name,' the stranger, now Ned, said, holding up the palm of his hand to fend off her anger. 'Mr Ned Browning. A fine name. I will do my best to make it a respectable one.'

'See that you do,' she ordered with a sisterly scold. 'I've christened you and any dishonor you bring to that name, you also bring to me.'

Serious young lady, 'Ned' thought as the girl turned to go. He could not have seen the smile she carried with her from the small room. Better just being a 'Ned', Tess Bright was thinking. His real name was probably Hezekiah Pybomoski. Walking along the narrow hallway toward the kitchen she was intercepted by her father.

'How is he?' Orson Bright asked in his slow out-country drawl.

'Better,' Tess answered. 'He's alert and talking.'

'Talking about what?'

'The weather. He hasn't gotten his memory back, Father, if that's what you were wondering. He asked me to give him a name.'

'Did you?' Orson asked, staring down at his

daughter as if it were an unwonted intimacy.

'I did!' Tess shot back. 'What's the harm in it?'

'None,' Orson answered, He scratched his bristled cheek, waiting.

'Ned Browning. I decided to name him that,' Tess said. Then she brushed past her father, carrying the tray to the kitchen where Mother Rose sang old West Virginia hill songs softly as she cleaned. Orson went out to the smoky front room where Andy Bright sat brooding in the near-darkness.

'I'm ready to put it to him, Andy,' Orson said. 'Do you want to be there?'

Andy nodded and rose heavily from his puncheon chair, a knitted shawl over his shoulders, a Colt revolver dangling on his hip.

Tess had reappeared from the kitchen, a soapy tress she had tried to sweep back from her forehead nearly draped over one eye. She placed her hands on her hips and demanded, 'What are you two playing at?' Her eyes went from her brother to her father, an expression near menace lighting them.

'What's it to you?' Andy Bright asked sullenly. He stood with his hands deep in the pockets of his twill pants, eyes downcast.

'Father?'

'It's nothing, Tess. Nothing to concern yourself with. We just want to talk to the man, that's all.'

'Why him? Why Ned?'

'*Ned?*' Andy Bright said, his hands clenching. 'Has he remembered his name, then?'

'No,' Tess said, surprised by her brother's vehemence. Andy's big hands relaxed slightly. He glanced at Orson, got a reassuring smile in return and apologized to Tess.

'That's all right then. I'm sorry.'

'You don't want him to remember anything, do you?' Tess asked, frowning. 'But why, Father.'

Orson patted her shoulder paternally. 'You don't need to know,' he said waving a dismissive hand.

'But I would like to,' she insisted. 'It has something to do with all the recent trouble with Colbert, hasn't it? You want to use him . . . Ned . . . for something.'

'If I do,' Orson said hotly, his anger resurfacing, 'it's for the benefit of all of us, for the family. I don't want you talking to him anymore, to *Ned*. Nothing but good morning and how are you, do you understand?

'No,' Tess said doubtfully. 'But,' she went on,

speaking as a dutiful daughter, 'I will do as you wish, Father.'

'Fine,' Orson said, his bony hand still resting on his daughter's shoulder. 'Then we'll leave it at that. Forget about Ned, he is in my hands now. I don't intend to trick him into anything that's shameful. I'll promise you that.'

'All right,' Tess answered quietly, letting her eyes meet his. She had trusted this man to guide her life for the first twenty years; she must trust him also in this one decision although she did not understand it entirely. Brushing his bristled cheek with her lips, she turned and went back into the kitchen, leaving Orson and his son alone.

'She's gettin' to where she could use a whippin' from time to time,' Andy Bright said.

'Yes,' Orson drawled thoughtfully, looking at the closed kitchen door. 'But then she's also a little bit too grown-up for that.'

'Half a woman, half a little girl,' Andy agreed in a dull voice. Orson stared at his hulking, unimaginative son.

Half a man, half a spoiled overgrown boy, Orson thought, but did not say. He looped his scrawny arm over his son's bearlike shoulders and reminded Andy, 'Let me do all of the talking,

Andy. I've got it all thought out, and you adding anything might fuddle things.'

'All right,' Andy agreed instantly. The truth was he had not come up with a single thing he might contribute in a conversation with 'Ned', and he was perfectly willing to remain silent while his father explained things to the stranger – and to Andy! Orson had something in mind, something important, that was clear, but exactly how he intended to go about matters was a mystery to the bulky young man. In silence he followed Orson to the stranger's bedroom. Adjusting his face into a smile, Orson Bright rapped three times on the plank door. They were immediately summoned in.

The stranger sat bare-chested on the bed. He had managed to step into his trousers, and was now making heavy work of pulling his boots on.

'Good morning, sir,' he said amiably. He tugged at his boots again, wincing with the effort. 'Well, Ned, how are you?'

The stranger cocked his head and smiled at the use of the adopted name. 'So Tess told you that she has christened me.'

'Yes,' Orson said affably, seating himself on the bed beside the young stranger. 'It's for the best.'

29

Orson Bright's eyes met Ned's and then lowered. 'There's no point in having her know your real name, is there?'

Ned tried to read the old man's intent, but could not. Something in the back of his mind raised a cautious head and growled a muted warning. Ned could not have said what the internal warning meant; he was having more of those episodes as the day grew older. Memory, trying with enormous effort to bring him back to himself, and failing with each try.

'You ... know who I am?' He asked Orson carefully. The old man's face lit up with mock astonishment.

'Of course, boy! Of course. Wasn't it I who sent for you? Damn ... you can't even remember that much, can you?'

'No, sir,' Ned answered as if shamed by the admission, 'I cannot recall even that much.'

Orson Bright's expression grew solemn. 'And with all the money I sent you!' Orson said dismally. Ned had risen shakily to his feet, and Orson Bright told his son: 'Take one of your shirts out of the closet, Andy. Help the man dress himself.'

Andy obeyed mutely and withdrew a faded

30

dark-blue shirt from the closet to clothe Ned. Buttoning the shirt, Ned raised downcast eyes to the lanky Orson Bright. 'You paid me money to do some sort of work for you, is that right?'

'Of course,' Orson said with evident frustration 'Two hundred dollars sent to you in Leesville. I don't know if you spent it, lost it or—'

'I don't even know where Leesville is,' Ned said, tucking his shirt tails in.

'But you know where you are now?'

'Only by what Tess told me.'

'God's sake man!' Andy said, unable to control himself. 'We paid you, you accepted the job. Why do you think you are here now? How did you make your way here?' the boy asked.

Orson Bright quieted Andy's outburst with a withering look. Andy was on the right track now, but his assistance was not called for.

'I made my way here . . .' Ned muttered, still searching for the lost voices in his mind. He wandered to the sun-bright window, seated himself in a ladder-backed wooden chair and let the warmth of morning bathe him in a flickering, golden glow. 'Mr Bright,' he said, 'I do not know who I am or what task I agreed to perform, but I feel that . . . I *am* a man of my word. Tell me what project you have engaged me on, and I promise you that I will do my best to perform the task, assuming of course, that I can recall the requisite skills.'

'Huh?' said Andy who was often confused with words of more than two syllables. Orson sighed, directing the expression at Andy Bright and Ned equally. *A fine pair,* he seemed to be thinking.

'I'm assuming that you have retained your necessary skills,' Orson Bright said, walking nearer to Ned, covering him with his narrow shadow. 'A gunman doesn't forget how to draw his Colt and dispense frontier justice.'

THREE

Orson Bright continued to speak. He had crossed the floor of the small room in order to toe the door shut for privacy. Now he rubbed his white hair, gestured with a nod for Andy to take a seat on the rumpled bed, and himself leaned against the rough wall of the room, arms folded, watching Ned Browning seriously.

'Mister . . .' he began and then clamped his jaw shut. A moment later he continued: 'I don't know what to say to you. Your credentials are well known across Wyoming. When you agreed to take care of this little matter for us, we considered that we had spent a lot of money, but expected in return to have a true professional coming to assist us. Now,' he said, waving an agitated hand, 'we find ourselves saddled with a man who not only does not seem able to remember our proposition, nor who he even is, but has given an indication that he does not recall receiving payment for the work and therefore has no obligation to perform it!'

'I didn't say that,' Ned answered promptly but faintly. 'It's just that—'

'It's just that you have no memory of payment, promises made or obligation to us.'

'It's just,' Ned said holding his head in both hands, 'that I have no memory of anything at all.'

'None?' Orson said, his voice rising. 'No idea of who you are and how you just happened to find your way to my place in a territory of nearly a hundred-thousand square miles?'

'No,' Ned said, lifting tormented eyes.

Orson threw his hands into the air. 'So then my money is lost – simply lost! Do you have any idea how hard it is to save two hundred dollars, how much labor and thrift it demands? And then to put all of our hopes in you, mister . . . all of our hopes of surviving.'

'If I could only—' Ned began, but it was just then that Tess opened the door, saw her father stalking the floor, her brother sagged onto the bed, Ned sitting like a witness being interrogated in a courtroom.

'I just wondered—' she said. A look from her father silenced her. Something, she knew intuitively, was going on – something of great importance. But it was a secret thing among the men. They would tell her when they wished her to know. Her dark-blue eyes met those of Ned Browning and a look passed between them that was questioning and reassuring at once. 'I see it's not the right time,' she said with a faint, nearly heartsick smile and turned away from the door.

'Her too!' Orson Bright said. The old man was no fool. He had intercepted and analyzed the look that had traveled between his daughter and Ned. 'Can you imagine what it would be like for a young woman like Tess to be without food, warmth or home when winter comes? Is she to wander the wastelands when the snow falls, with savages like Santana prowling the winterscape?'

'I don't—' was all Ned was able to murmur.

'I wasn't thinking only of my land, my pride, myself when I sent that message to Leesville, sir! I was thinking of my family! Of Andy here, of Mother Rose . . . of Tess.' He lowered his head and turned away. 'I will hold you to no bargain. Circumstances, I see, are extraordinary. Heal, rest and then go on your way, mister ... Ned Browning. We shall suffer our fate as we must. It was a forlorn and desperate hope that encouraged me to seek your help. I can see now that I should have only trusted the Lord ... and pocketed my two hundred dollars.' These last few words were delivered in a pulpit tone. Whether they were intended to shame Ned or not, they had that effect. A family trusting him – counting on him – whoever he was! For their salvation. Perhaps it was because he was still so confused, perhaps out of a sense of honor. Perhaps because of Tess with the blue eyes that he shook himself drew a deep breath and rose from the wooden chair.

He asked, 'Tell me again what the situation is, and let's try to find a solution.'

Orson Bright had seated himself on the foot of the bed, facing Ned who still stood at the window. Andy Bright, easily bored and willing to get back to his hard labors, had picked up his hat and walked out, leaving the two men alone in the closed, sunlit room.

'Ten years ago,' Orson Bright began, 'I came into the Tumano Basin. The Shoshone Indians still had not been pacified and we were forted up much of the time, trying to defend the little we had. There was an outlaw called Santana roving the timberlands too. He claimed to be Indian-Mexican, but I doubt if he knew himself what he was or where he came from. He left us alone for the most part until a few years back.'

'What happened?' Ned asked.

'He and my older son, Dan, got into it over something down in the town of Hoyt's Camp. What it was, I never knew for sure.' Orson shook his head and licked his lips. 'A woman, they tell me. Who she was, what happened to her, I can't say. I can't even swear that it's true.

'We, as a family, fought on, however. You can see the timber resources here. Lodgepole pines, jack pines, cedar. All plentiful hereabouts. And the money is good – down-river, beyond Hoyt's Camp, they're building little settlements nearby as quick as they can saw lumber.'

'Then?' Ned prompted.

'Then we prospered for a time, after years of doing without the basics of life. But a man named Lyle Colbert moved in below us. He figured how to make himself a lot of money without the back-breaking effort that timbering requires.'

37

'Namely?' Ned interrupted. He was interested, but his wounds had sapped his energy and, seating himself again in the ladder-back chair, he felt as if he would drowse off before Orson Bright reached the end of his tale. Bright seemed to sense that; he rushed on.

'What Colbert has done, Ned, is throw a chain across the river. Two-inch thick steel the links have, and he won't lower it for our timber rafts unless we pay a toll. A heavy toll,' Orson said unhappily. 'Now we've got only my son, Andy, and two hired loggers working the timber. Three other men quit because I couldn't afford to pay them full wages. It's gotten to this. I'll go broke and be forced from my land, leaving the timber to Colbert – which is what he wants – or we declare war on him and drive him and his river pirates from the Snake.'

'Which brings us to the reason you sent for me,' Ned said, looking up.

'Which brings us to that point.'

'How do you propose to fight Colbert?' Ned asked. 'And how many men has he with him?'

'As to how many men he has, it varies. Between ten and thirty, I would estimate.' Orson hesitated and said sincerely, 'As to how to fight him – well, that's your business, isn't it? That's what you have been paid to figure out.'

'Yes,' Ned said dully. That was what he had been paid for. He wondered what he had done with the money. He wondered if he – in his normal, resourceful state of mind – would have grinned, produced a cunning scheme, a plan of action against which Lyle Colbert and his river rats would have no answer. Just now he, Ned Browning, had not even the vaguest idea of how to go about this piece of work. Just now he had trouble even focusing his eyes on the narrowly built old man standing before him: Orson Bright who had entrusted all of his savings to `Ned' and waited anxiously for a solution to his woes.

'I'll start looking around tomorrow,' Ned told Bright. 'I'm still feeling poorly. I shouldn't have been so eager to climb out of that bed.'

'I understand, son,' Bright said. 'You're no good to us if you're not feeling at full strength. You get your rest. I'll have Tess bring you another tray of food.'

Ned nodded his appreciation. Starting toward the door, Orson paused and said, 'Ned, I'd appreciate it if you didn't discuss the particulars of our agreement with Tess. Let the girl think that your coming here was nothing more than an accident. She doesn't need to know, or to carry extra worries with her.'

'Mr Bright . . . what is my real name?' Ned Browning asked.

'Why, it's Lavender, Frank Lavender,' Orson replied. He had chosen the name of a well-known gunfighter at random. Frank Lavender was a bad man; Frank Lavender had also been hung two months earlier. It seemed to satisfy the wounded man who shrugged and said:

'I guess it's best if we keep calling me Ned Browning . . . for the girl's sake. Besides, no one else needs to know I am here.'

'You're right, Frank . . . Ned,' Orson Bright agreed. He closed the door softly behind him and smiled, congratulating himself on his fortune. Orson had actually considered hiring a gunfighter to help him in his battle with Lyle Colbert, but he was cash poor and the idea had seemed chancy at best anyway. Now he had a man willing to fight for him and, more, one who would not ask for money to do the work! Orson Bright considered himself both fortunate and ingeniously clever at that moment. He whistled tunelessly as he went out onto the front porch of his small cabin, stretched and thought: *Welcome, Frank Lavender*. He chuckled and went out into the yard to feed his horses.

Ned was still feeling very weak the following morning. He walked out to breakfast with the Bright family, dizzy and feeling fragile. He eased himself onto a plank bench next to Orson, across from Tess. Andy, bullish and rough-looking for a man so young, had his sleeves rolled up as if for clearance as he dug into his hotcakes. Ned waved Mother Rose's offer of food aside and contented himself with a cup of dark, strong coffee. Andy threw his napkin onto the table and spoke up, 'You'd better start eating if you mean to keep your strength up.'

Ned didn't reply. Orson Bright told his son: 'It's hard to eat when you got no appetite, Andy. Soon as he's well, he'll eat like a horse.'

'When's that going to be?' Andy Bright demanded. 'We need him now!'

Tess stared blankly first at her brother then at Ned Browning. Need Ned for what?

'He'll be ready,' Orson said soothingly as he sipped at his own coffee. 'Won't you . . . Ned?'

What was going on here, Tess continued to

wonder, even after Orson and Andy had gone off to the timberlands to check on the work crew and Mother Rose to scrub down the kitchen. Ned sat on a rickety chair on the front porch of the cabin, letting the warmth of the sun soothe his wounded arm. The pleasant morning did nothing to ease the confusion the blow to his head had caused. Tess emerged from the house and sat on the steps of the porch, her arms looped around her knees, watching the sun slant through the trees and the distant silver glitter of the river. A group of crows had taken up a position in the high branches of a deep blue-green lodgepole pine and they watched the strutting, complaining birds for a time in silence.

'What do they want you to do?' Tess finally asked without turning her head.

'It's not real clear,' Ned said with a hint of a smile.

'Fight?'

'That was the idea I got,' Ned Browning answered. Now Tess did turn her eyes on him. She shifted her palms to the porch as if she were about to rise.

'You can't do that,' she said in a very low voice strained with concern. 'You're not well.'

'I'm healing.'

'Then heal. Just don't get well enough to get yourself killed.'

'Who's going to kill me?' Ned asked.

'You don't know Lyle Colbert. If you get in his way, he'll surely kill you. Why would you want to get involved in our troubles anyway?'

'I don't *want* to,' Ned told the girl. 'It's a matter of obligation.' He hesitated. 'I owe your family.'

'For what? Fishing you out of the river?' Tess asked hotly. She did rise now to stand before him, her hands on her hips. Since apparently Orson had told his daughter nothing about the bargain he had made with Frank Lavender, he did not elaborate.

'It's just something I have to do.'

'Why!' Tess asked pleadingly. She spread her hands in frustration. 'Why do you men have to traipse around trying to get yourselves killed? What is the matter with you? Why?'

'I already told you – I have an obligation. That means a lot to me. Why would I back out now?'

'Because . . .' her words stammered from her lips, 'because I don't want you to! I don't want to see you hurt again.'

With that, Tess swept off the porch toward the

deep forest, holding her blue skirt high. Ned Browning sighed and sat there in deep thought for a while before re-entering the house. Mother Rose only glanced at him as he sat at the table and began disassembling a Colt revolver – it had been Dan Bright's weapon – that Orson had left for him.

That morning before departing Andy Bright had asked Ned Browning, 'Are you going to file the action down? I heard a lot of you . . . a lot of men like to have a hair-trigger on their pistols.'

'I don't see the use in that,' Ned had answered. 'It just raises the risk of you shooting yourself in the foot before you have even cleared leather.'

How Ned had come by that piece of knowledge, he could not have answered. Any more than he could explain how he knew every piece of the pistol, how to disassemble, reassemble, clean with the brass brush and oil the Colt so that its action was silky and sure.

Of course, in his previous life as Frank Lavender, he must certainly have been familiar with weapons. He supposed there are some things a man doesn't forget even when most of his past is a complete blank.

Tess had returned. He glanced up at her and

smiled. She paid as much attention to him as she would have to a piece of furniture. Beyond the open door, the crows rose in unison and flew away. Ned Browning sat at the table with his head in both hands, wanting, needing to remember.

'All right, boys,' Orson Bright was saying to his two-man logging crew, 'we start rolling the timber downslope and work it up onto the barge.'

'What's the point?' Amos Shockley, the larger of the two, asked, looking up from his end of the long, sharp-toothed saw. 'We can't get anything downriver past Colbert's chain.'

'The point is that I told you to do it,' Orson said with a show of temper. 'Unless you don't want to get paid.'

'It's August and we ain't been paid since June,' the other man, the wiry Bert Smart said, standing up from the two-man saw to mop his perspiring brow. 'Of course we want to get paid, but what guarantee is there that we ever will?'

'You will,' Orson promised. 'We're getting downriver to Hoyt's Camp this time.'

'Just how are we going to do that?' Amos Shockley asked in a mocking tone. The bearded man was challenging on this morning, and Orson understood that not being paid had stuck in the craws of these, the last two men of his original five-man logging crew.

'We've got help,' young Andy Bright said, pushing his horse's head aside as he stepped belligerently toward Shockley who stood his ground.

'Help?' Shockley said looking around the empty forest where one out of every dozen trees had been reduced to a stump as a result of their summer's labor. 'Mind telling me where they are?'

'You can believe me,' Orson Bright said mildly, not wanting the discussion to go further. Andy had clenched his fists, looking ready to fight.

Shockley smiled at Andy, studied his aggressive stance and spat. 'You're a big pup, Andy, I'll give you that. But you're only a pup.'

'Hold on, both of you,' Orson pleaded. 'Just trust me. We've found help.'

'I asked you to show me,' Amos Shockley said. Now Bert Smart stepped beside his bulkier friend and took his elbow, trying to calm the big man.

'We'll show you, all right!' young Andy Bright said triumphantly playing his trump card. 'Or haven't you ever heard of Frank Lavender?'

46

Orson winced. He had not wanted the kid to blurt out the name like that, had hoped to reassure his unpaid loggers without invoking the legendary gunfighter's name.

'Are you saying that Frank Lavender is here?' Bert Smart asked with disbelief.

'That's what I said,' Andy replied with heat.

'Why would a man like that get involved in our fight?' big Amos Shockley asked. 'How could you meet his price when you can't even afford our wages?'

'It's a private matter,' Orson replied. 'The man owes me a favor.'

'This does change matters, Amos,' the narrow Bert Smart said.

'If it's so.' Amos Shockley was dubious. The two of them had been about ready to give notice and hit the road looking for work that paid actual money. But if Frank Lavender was actually in the mix – well, that did change things.

'It's my sister,' Andy said, embellishing the situation. 'Frank's crazy for her. He offered to help us out.'

'Frank Lavender?' Amos scoffed. 'When could he have ever met Tess? She's hardly ever even been off the property.'

47

'Well, she goes into Hoyt's Camp for supplies,' Andy said, continuing to lie, quite proud of his powers of invention. 'That's where he met her. Just now he's down in our cabin, greasing up his guns.'

'I heard that Lavender was dead,' Bert Smart said. Andy sneered at the narrow logger.

'Yes? You want to go down there and say that to him? He's alive, all right, and Lyle Colbert hasn't got enough guns or the nerve to stop Frank Lavender. Now let's get started loading those logs on the barge. We're going downriver.'

FOUR

Ned Browning awoke early from a series of troubled dreams. The sun was still only a chill orange glow through the ranks of the pine and cedar trees, glinting off the small window of his bedroom when he started awake and sat up in bed so rapidly that it caused his injured shoulder to flare with pain.

The dreams. In them he was surrounded by men wearing badges, men without faces, in what seemed to be a jailhouse . . . and then they were gone, disappearing like smoke, and he was riding alone out on a far land without form or substance, pursued by ghosts. He fell then, twisting and rolling through a long dark tunnel. . . .

There was no more that he could remember.

49

Rising uneasily he walked to the window and peered out at the new morning. There were cottontail rabbits nibbling at the young grass, mockingbirds and sparrows flitting around aimlessly, the flock of brooding black crows in the heights of the single tree they seemed to prefer.

Ned sagged back onto the bed. He sat there trying to make some sense of the dream, to relate it to his present reality. It seemed to him that Orson Bright must have been correct. He must have been the outlaw Frank Lavender, arrested for some crime. Then, perhaps, he had somehow broken free only to be shot down in the escape attempt. It fit the pieces of the dream puzzle together, but it did not *feel* like the truth. That is, he did not feel himself to be a gunman, an outlaw, a killer. He touched the back of his skull where the painful knot still bulged, blocking his memory.

Slowly, carefully, he began to dress himself. He liked none of what Orson Bright had in mind for him, yet if he had given his word, taken the timberman's money . . . he strapped on the holstered belt Orson had given him and slipped the newly oiled Colt from it, feeling its weight in his hand, the balance of the weapon. It was not an unfamiliar instrument, he recognized with a frown. Returning it to the holster, he looked at himself in the mirror and drew the weapon as rapidly as possible. Before a man could have blinked, the pistol was leveled, the hammer of the gun drawn back. Perhaps that should have been a comforting experiment, but it depressed Ned Browning.

Yes, he was a man born to the gun, skilled in its use. That much was obvious, but it was far from heartening. It was only another mark on the dark side of the ledger, one more indication that he was indeed a man who hired out to kill for other men.

Frank Lavender.

No one was yet at the table for breakfast when he walked out, passed directly through to the front door and stepped outside into the pre-dawn. The pine trees were richly fragrant. He could smell the river, hear it as it boiled past. A pair of squirrels leaped among the branches of a cedar tree, chattering as they played. Ned found no pleasure in watching them, nor in the bite of the cool morning air, the sight of the long wooded slopes.

He did not belong here, in a situation like this.

How he knew that he could not have said, but he felt that he did not. Yet where was he to go? If it was true that he was a wanted man on the run, a man who could not tell his friends from his enemies and had no idea where safe ground lay, what was the use in fleeing?

'You're up early.'

Ned turned to find Tess behind him, a small bundle of wood in her arms. Her blue eyes sparkled mysteriously in the early morning light. Her blond hair was loose across her shoulders. She seemed ready to smile, but held the expression back.

'Couldn't sleep,' Ned answered. 'Let me help you with that wood.'

He took the small bundle from her arms. Standing that near to her he could smell the lye soap on her and a more distant, softer fragrance like lilac. She watched him with those intent blue eyes. Tess's mouth moved again, as if to ask a question, but like her smile, she managed to repress the words.

'I like to get the stove fire started before Mother Rose gets up. She has enough work to do cooking for us all.'

They tramped up onto the cabin porch as the

first golden rays of dawn light struck the tips of the tall trees. Inside the cabin it was still cool and dark. 'What can I do?' Ned asked after dumping the firewood into the iron cradle provided for it.

'Nothing, I don't suppose,' Tess said. Now her eyes seemed to settle on his hip, as if only now had she become aware that he was wearing a sidearm. Her look was not disapproving, but anxious. 'Are you well enough to go out?' she asked.

'To go out?'

'Yes. To . . . well . . . what would you call it? Go to work?'

'I don't know,' Ned Browning said, seating himself on a wooden chair which he turned toward the stove to watch Tess at her task. 'I feel pretty useless just lying around in bed, though. I thought I could at least go out and look things over. I'd like to see how Lyle Colbert is set up, maybe take a look at Hoyt's Camp.'

'I'll take you,' Tess said, keeping her back to him as she struck a second match, trying to start the tinder in the iron stove.

'You?'

'I have to take the buckboard into Hoyt's Camp today to purchase some necessities – if our credit is still any good at the general store.' The last

53

words were tightly expelled between grimly set lips. Things could not have been easy out here with no market for the Brights' timber. 'If only you had come sooner,' Tess said, turning to face him now, her arms folded beneath her breasts, her back propped against the zinc tub beside the stove. The fire had begun to flicker to life. A few golden sparks escaped into the room and Tess closed the door to the stove.

'If I had come sooner?' Ned said curiously.

'You know, when you were supposed to arrive, before Lyle Colbert had gathered those rough men of his and laid the chain across the Snake.'

'You know, then,' Ned said. 'Why I am here, I mean.'

'I heard Father and Andy talking. I know who you are now. Frank Lavender, isn't that right?'

'So they tell me,' Ned could only answer. He smiled when he said it, but there was not much humor behind the admission. The small girl walked two paces from the stove and stood looking down at him. Her eyes seemed troubled now. Her lip trembled slightly before she spoke.

'I am going to continue to call you Ned. Is that all right? It is the name I christened you with, and I like it much better than Frank Lavender.'

54

The team had been hitched to the buckboard, Tess in her blue dress, assisted up onto the bench seat when a sulky Andy Bright rode through the pines to rein up roughly beside them.

'You going to Hoyt's Camp?' he demanded.

'That's right,' Tess told her bull-necked brother.

'I'm going with you. You can't be riding off alone with a man.'

'Did Dad tell you to ride along?' Tess demanded, pulling on her driving gloves.

'That doesn't matter!' Andy Bright said. 'I'm going to town with you.'

'You're not needed ... or wanted,' Tess said, unwinding the reins from the brake handle.

Ned Browning spoke up, 'It doesn't matter, does it, Tess? Andy might be of some help to me.'

'If you say so,' Tess said sharply. She loosed the brake, snapped the reins against the rumps of the two-horse team and guided them forward along the mountain trail, followed by her surly brother on his shaggy buckskin horse. 'I didn't want him to come along,' she said to Ned Browning after a silent half-mile of driving.

'I know that,' he said. 'But there's no sense in squabbling over it.'

'I love Andy, he's my brother. It's just that sometimes I get so tired of seeing him around.'

'It's always like that between brothers and sisters or brothers and brothers,' Ned commented as they passed through the depths of the forest, cool and dark where they traveled, sun-bright in the upper reaches of the trees.

Ned said, 'Let me know when you see Lyle Colbert's place. I'd like to look it over.'

'You're planning on going ahead, then? With Father's plan?' she asked with concern.

'What else can I do?'

'Besides getting yourself killed, you mean? I can think of a lot of things!'

Andy Bright, still sullen, followed them closely. The young man was carrying a grudge, but Ned Browning was not exactly sure who, or what, he held it against. Maybe life itself.

Eventually they emerged from the forest and Tess slowed and then halted the team on a hill overlooking the long valley below. In the distance to the north was the town of Hoyt's Camp, founded, if that was the right word, by an early settler, a fur trader who had first camped there to escape the dreadful high-mountain winters. There was the river rambling past, and long grassy plains. It hadn't taken other westward-bound travelers long to find the pretty little place.

'To the south,' Tess said, pointing, 'right on the edge of the river. That's Lyle Colbert's outfit.'

What Ned could see of the camp through the scattered trees was a collection of rough log cabins, thrown up without pattern or planning. Shelter from the hard weather, quickly erected. Beyond these was a single larger building, also of log, but more carefully built. It had a peaked roof unlike the smaller cabins. There seemed to be several outbuildings of sawn wood and a corral farther along. It was difficult to make out the details. Andy Bright had been sitting his buckskin beside the wagon. Now Ned Browning asked, 'Where is the chain, Andy?'

'You can't see it from here,' Andy said, still scowling. 'It's a few hundred yards downriver. What do you intend to do about it, Lavender?'

'Don't call him that,' Tess said, but neither man seemed to hear her.

'I haven't had the time to give it a lot of thought,' Ned Browning replied, shifting his eyes from the river to meet Andy's dark gaze. 'Before anything else is done against Colbert, I believe it's essential that we remove the chain.'

'How are you going to do that?' Andy demanded in his bitter way. 'Bite through it?'

'Look,' Ned said, with a patience he was not feeling, 'it can be easily done. How is the chain anchored?'

Andy blinked and said dully, 'Padlocked around a five-foot-thick pine.'

'That figures,' Ned replied. He gave a half-shrug and rubbed his sore left shoulder thoughtfully. 'What is it that you men do for a living?'

Andy scowled. 'You know what we do. We're timbermen.'

'Have you ever seen a tree you couldn't fell?' Ned asked.

'No,' Andy said defensively.

'Well, that one,' Ned said, lifting his chin toward the river, 'is just another task. Take it down to a stump and throw the chain off it.'

Andy laughed sarcastically. 'And you think Lyle Colbert is going to just stand by and watch.'

'No,' Ned said, frowning himself now. 'That is the tricky part of the plan, isn't it? We'll have to come up with an idea to distract Lyle Colbert's men.'

Andy laughed again, this time with outrageous mockery. 'That is why you've been brought here! To tell us the obvious? That we have to remove the chain! Lavender, you're a genius,' Andy said and heeled his horse downslope through the trees toward the town of Hoyt's Camp.

'Don't mind him, Ned,' Tess said quietly as she restarted the team.

'I don't. He has a point. I was just stating the obvious, but remember I just arrived here. I have to learn a lot more about matters before leaping with both feet into what could be a bloody quagmire.'

Neither of them spoke for a long time, until they emerged onto the flatlands where tall August grass waved in the scented breeze off of the mountain slopes. Ned pondered silently, but his thoughts were not on Lyle Colbert's chain and the battle which might lay ahead, but on the nape of Tess's neck where a loose curl had escaped to twist free, soft and golden in the summer breeze. He watched the intent look on her face, the pursed lips and anxious blue eyes of Tess Bright and decided that the girl was right – there were a lot of better ways for a man to spend his life than getting himself killed over a fight that was not even his own.

'Isn't there any local law here?' Ned asked as they approached outskirts of town.

'Only the sheriff over at Bainbridge. That's about twenty miles north.'

'Have your father, the other timbermen, considered taking their troubles to court?'

'Hire lawyers? With what money? And wait months for their case to be decided while they slowly go broke? No, I don't think they have considered that,' Tess said with a hint of irony. 'The others have continued to pay Colbert's exorbitant fees. Father refuses. He says that no man can own a section of the river and that Lyle Colbert is nothing but a pirate. He will not yield.'

'Instead, he sent for me,' Ned said.

'Yes.' Tess glanced at him as she slowed the team. 'And what can you do, Ned?'

'I don't know. I honestly have no idea what can be done . . . if anything.'

The town of Hoyt's Camp wasn't much to look at. The great majority of the structures were of unbarked logs, that having been the only building material in the days before the sawmill had been erected. There were more men and horses around than Ned Browning had expected, most of them idle. Tess told him without having been asked:

'Timbermen without any work to do if their employers aren't wealthy enough to pay Lyle Colbert's fees for river passage.'

'Where are you going?' he asked.

'To the general store over there,' she said nodding toward yet another log structure. 'To beg for credit. I'd rather not have you there watching me lower myself to it, if you don't mind.'

'Whatever you like.' They were just passing a low building where the sour smell of stale beer was heavy in the air, and the occasional shout of a man within could be heard. Tess frowned and pointed out her brother's buckskin among the row of horses tethered in front of the saloon.

'Andy's in there. You might as well go in as well and have a quiet drink.'

'If you say so,' Ned agreed as Tess halted the buckboard. He stepped up onto the plankwalk in front of the building and watched as Tess crossed the street to park the rig in front of the general store. After she had entered the building, he shrugged mentally and entered the smoky saloon.

Andy Bright had already had his quiet drink.

He was still drinking as Ned Browning entered the low-ceilinged building, but he was no longer quiet. A loose circle of men was standing around Andy, listening to him spout off, not soberly.

'. . . You'd all listen to me, we could run Lyle Colbert off his property and open the river up again. How else are we to make a living?'

A few men laughed, others stood listening intently, if dubiously. Two men seated at a round table across the saloon glared at Andy. Those two, Ned Browning realized, did not have the look of timbermen about them. They wore their revolvers low, and their shoulders were too narrow and their hands too soft-appearing. Andy Bright was continuing with his discourse. Ned decided that it was time to take the bull-headed kid out into the fresh air before trouble could start.

Before Ned could reach him, one of the two men rose from the round table and called out tauntingly: 'Hey kid! If you're thinking of trying to run Lyle Colbert off, you might as well start with me.'

There was a vicious smile on the sneering man's face. He wore a thin, dark mustache. His hand dangled loosely near his holster. The knot of men surrounding Andy Bright separated so that Andy had a clear view of the narrow man.

'You, Traylor! You think I'm afraid of you?' Andy said, not too wisely. He had just enough whiskey in his veins for false courage. The gunman's sneer did not alter.

'If you had any sense you would be,' the man called Traylor said, taking two steps forward.

The bystanders had faded away until they were nearly lined along the walls of the low building. Traylor eyed them, seeing no man who appeared ready to risk his life with Andy Bright.

'It looks as if you're playing a lone hand, Bright' Traylor said. Andy glanced around, concern showing in his eyes now. He had been doing a lot of talking, but he hadn't been prepared for the idea of actually starting a fight. Not this soon.

Andy's eyes flickered toward Ned Browning, halted there and then returned to Traylor. 'Not quite a lone hand,' Andy said, his confidence returning. Traylor's small eyes shifted to Ned Browning, took him in without apparent concern and focused again on Andy. The gunhand's friend had not bothered to rise to his feet. He sat at the table smiling, sipping at his whiskey.

'One more lumberjack doesn't frighten me,' Traylor said, spitting on the floor of the saloon.

'He should, you damn fool,' Andy said so that every man in the room could hear him. 'This "lumberjack" happens to be Frank Lavender!'

Ned Browning silently cursed. He supposed that he, too, would have to eventually tangle with men like Traylor, but he preferred it to be a time of his own choosing, not over a trifling bit of boasting in a saloon. Andy had been cautioned not to mention the name of Lavender, but fear or braggadocio, or both, had caused him to rope Ned into the fight.

Traylor shifted his attention again to Ned. He licked his lips. 'I don't believe you, Bright,' he said. Those were the last words he spoke before he went for his gun. They were the last words he ever was to speak. Ned had been ready for the Colbert man's draw. His own wrist twitched, his fingers snapped the Colt from its holster and before Traylor had brought his gun up, Ned's Colt roared.

The spinning .44 bullet caught Traylor's heart. Blood trickled from his mouth as he swayed on his feet for a moment before burying his face in the planking of the floor. The second Colbert rider had started to rise, but by then Ned Browning had shifted his sights that way and the man gave it up, raising his hands, his expression one of twisted, impotent rage.

'Get his pistol, Andy,' Ned Browning commanded, 'then let's get out of here.'

Andy Bright strode across the room, his bullish gait cocky, his hat tilted back. He lifted the Colbert man's pistol from its holster, backed away from him, paused to give the gathered timbermen a triumphant glance, tucked the pistol behind his belt and walked behind Ned to the green-painted door of the saloon.

Outside, the air was fresh, clean, cool. 'I knew you could handle things, Frank,' Andy said, clapping a hand on Ned Browning's shoulder.

'Next time keep your mouth shut,' Ned snapped. 'Get your horse.'

Several people had emerged from the surrounding buildings, summoned by the sound of the gunshot, Tess Bright was among them. She stood watching nervously from the porch of the general store. Ned started that way, alert for any sound or motion behind him. The Colbert rider they had disarmed had been stunned by the rapid turn of events, but Ned had no idea that the man was a coward. If he were, he would have chosen another way to make a living.

'What happened?' Tess asked as Ned stepped up onto the porch to join her. Her blue eyes were clouded with fear.

'Nothing,' Ned replied calmly, 'just a couple of troublemakers making noise. Did you get your supplies?'

Tess wore a frown. Glancing up the street she saw her brother walking his horse toward them, and that seemed to relieve her anxiety a little.

'All I could get,' she said, nodding toward the few provisions stacked in the buckboard's bed. 'I don't think there will be any credit for us here next time.'

'Let's hope you won't need any the next time you come,' Ned said with a confidence he did not feel. He saw now that Tess's hands were trembling. 'Do you want me to drive?'

'No!' she said somewhat defensively. 'It's my team. I know them, they know my touch.'

'Let's get going, then,' Ned suggested, and he helped her up onto the seat as Andy, flushed with excitement, rode up beside them.

'That was some shooting, Frank!' he said. 'You should have seen him, Sis. Royce Traylor never had a chance against Lavender's draw.'

Tess's mouth tightened. Ned glowered a warning at Andy who for once understood. Or maybe, Ned reflected, he had purchased the kid's respect with another man's blood.

It was not until they were well clear of the town, into the deep timber again, before Tess spoke, and when she did it was numbly, her eyes fixed on the trail ahead.

'A couple of troublemakers, huh? You killed a man back there, didn't you, Ned?'

'There wasn't a lot of choice.'

'There's always a choice,' Tess said, believing it. Ned didn't bother to reply. They were in sight of the Bright cabin before she added, 'It would have been better if you had never come here, Ned. They'll never let you leave alive. Not now.'

FIVE

Orson Bright and Andy tried to turn that evening's supper into a heroic banquet of sorts. Amos Shockley and Bert Smart had been invited down from their cabin in an apparent effort to bolster their spirits. Both of the lumberjacks looked uncomfortable, their hair slicked back, their shirts buttoned to the throat. Andy Bright regaled them with the tale of the shoot-out with Royce Traylor, stretching it out as if the fight had lasted hours. He repeatedly told the others how lightning-fast Frank Lavender was with a gun, as if by sharing the story enough he could bask in shared glory.

'There never was a faster man,' Andy concluded. Even Orson Bright who had been beaming at his son and his guests had grown tired of the tale before Mother Rose and Tess began serving the fresh-caught brook trout, red beans and cornbread with molasses that was their dinner.

The men ate silently for the most part, the ruddy, big-shouldered Amos Shockey eating everything that was placed in front of him, the narrow Bert Smart nearly keeping pace. Finally full, Shockley leaned back in his chair, his thick hands folded on his stomach.

'I guess it's a good thing for us that Lavender here met Tess,' he said affably but a little offensively. Tess had been clearing the platters away. Now she shot an unhappy glance at her brother, her father and Ned in turn, flushed slightly and scurried away to the sink where she dumped the dishes unceremoniously into the water. So, someone had been telling tales about her ... untrue tales. Mother Rose washed the dishes without a word, but she glanced at Tess and saw the annoyance there.

'Back in a minute,' Tess said, and she stepped through the kitchen toward the back storage area where she leaned against the wall, folded her arms and glowered fiercely.

Orson Bright was saying, 'So you see boys, I wasn't trying to string you along. We've got a chance of fighting our way through all of our problems now. Just keep loading the barge tomorrow. We'll soon be floating our timber downriver again, won't we, Frank?'

Ned nodded, dabbed at his mouth with a napkin and pushed away the bony remains of his fish. Something was expected of him and so he muttered, 'Sure we will, Mr Bright.' Unexpectedly he rose then and said, 'If you boys will excuse me. I'm still kind of beat up, and I think I'll turn in early.'

'No whiskey, Frank?' Orson Bright asked, bringing up a jug from under the table as Mother Rose began serving coffee all around.

'Never when I'm working,' Ned said. He looked around for Tess, did not see her and, nodding to the others, started for his room.

Lying on the bed, the bed that had belonged to Orson Bright's dead son, Dan, Ned Browning clasped his hands behind his bed and stared at the ceiling. Beyond the door the men's humor seemed to be improving as the evening wore on.

What now? Ned asked himself. How far did his obligation toward Orson Bright go? He had killed a man today only because of that promise, a promise he could not even remember making.

Ned had proven two things to himself on that day
– for one, he *was* good with a gun. The other was
that he had no taste for killing. He did not even
know the man he had shot down. Of course,
Royce Traylor had drawn on him, but that did not
mean that Ned felt justified in the shooting, that
he felt any sense of triumph in having survived
after having sent a man to his grave. Maybe Tess
had been right.

Maybe there was always another way.

Always a choice.

He closed his eyes and tried to sleep, but sleep
would not come. He listened to the muffled
voices of the men at their whiskey and continued
to stare at the low ceiling as the long hours
passed.

Tess could not remain forever in the storage
room. She did not wish to return to the table
where the men spoke. The eyes of the timbermen
would now turn toward her, wondering how well
she knew Frank Lavender, how intimately. She
had become a scrap of gossip, of amused
speculation and after Andy's lies – she could
throttle him for that – she couldn't say that any
such intimacy was complete fabrication. Rather,

she could, but she would not be believed. The story would get around the valley, of course. She was now the killer Frank Lavender's lover, or would be in the common mind. She wished again that Ned had never come into her life.

'Grab me a rag, Tess!' Mother Rose called. 'I sloshed some water on the floor.'

'All right.'

Resignedly, Tess went to the rag bag in the corner of the tiny room and searched for something suitable. The first cloth her fingers tightened around and extracted proved to be a familiar one. It was the red shirt that Ned Browning had been wearing when they had first pulled him from the river. She started to jam it back in the bag in disgust, but hesitated. The shirt was the only tangible evidence they had of Ned Browning's true identity. She turned the torn shirt around in her hands, remembering what Mother Rose had cautioned them about on that first night.

The brass grommets on the shirt's front, above the left breast, Rose had told them, could only have one possible use – to keep a badge from tearing the cloth. Tess fingered the small brass eyelets. Who then was Ned Browning? She knew that they had lied to him when they informed him that he was Frank Lavender, lied when they had told him that he owed them a favor as they had lied to Shockley and Bert Smart when they told the timbermen that the reason for the obligation was because Lavender was enamored of Tess.

Ned seemed to remain convinced that he owed something to Tess's father; no one had told her why that was. Probably, she considered, they had lied to him to convince him that it was so. Tess leaned against the wall, her fingertips briefly tracing patterns on her forehead.

It was all a lie! Every bit of it.

The only evidence of who Ned might be was the shirt, and Mother Rose believed it could only belong to a lawman. Poor Ned, he was as confused as she was – more so! She mentally apologized for being sharp with him, for remaining aloof. She wished that she could go into his room and talk to him now, but it was late; he was probably asleep, besides she was not going to pass the men and enter Frank Lavender's bedroom while they watched and speculated freely.

'Tess! What are you doing, girl? I'm standing in water!'

'Sorry,' Tess said. She grabbed another rag from the sack and without real reason folded the red shirt and tucked it behind the shelves which held various household items. There must be some way. Some way to help Ned Browning remember. Before things got much worse.

Morning was cool and bright. Ned Browning had been lying up in bed, enjoying the warmth of his blankets. From time to time his shoulder flared up with pain, but it was faint, only a reminder of his wound and not an urgent plea for relief. His aching head was a different story. Again he had awakened with the optimistic expectation that his memory might have returned during the night, only to be disappointed by the lack of same. Maybe, he thought with unhappy reflection, it would never return and he would remain Frank Lavender – or alternately, Ned Browning – for the rest of his life.

Bootsteps rang heavily on the front porch and a fist was thumped impatiently against the door. Orson Bright could be heard crossing the outer room, answering with impatience. Ned slipped from his bed, smoothed back his hair with one hand and planted his hat with the other. Buckling on his gunbelt, he proceeded to the front room to find Bright speaking with two new arrivals. They all glanced his way as he entered the room.

The fire was already going in the stove, Ned saw, and coffee was just beginning to boil. Andy Bright, sleep-rumpled, had emerged from his bedroom. Orson was speaking:

'The coffee'll be ready in a few minutes, boys. Sit down, won't you?'

The two newcomers did not remove their hats as they seated themselves, nor did they let their eyes wander far from Ned. They were both heavy-set, sun-burned men with wary expressions. Mother Rose had come in to start pouring the morning coffee.

'Sit down, Frank,' Orson Bright said. 'let me introduce you.'

Ned nodded and sagged onto the wooden bench opposite the two new arrivals, tilting his hat back. Coffee was placed before him; he nodded his thanks to Mother Rose. Tess was nowhere to be seen, although she must be around somewhere since one of her chores was to start the morning fire.

'These here are Billy Lofton and Mack Paulsen from the timber camps across the river. Boys, this is Frank Lavender.' All three men nodded. No one offered a hand. Andy stood away from the table, leaning against the wall, one heel up behind him.

'What can I do for you boys?'

'That's what we're here to find out,' the smaller of the two, Billy Lofton answered. 'We heard you had hired on some help. We want to know if anyone has come up with a plan to get us out of our predicament.'

'We just can't afford to hold on much longer,' Mack Paulsen chipped in.

'How did you two cross the river?' Ned asked unexpectedly.

'In our canoe, of course. There ain't no other way.'

Andy Bright glanced hopefully at Frank. The night had not diminished his newfound respect for Lavender. 'What are you thinking, Frank?'

Ned took a sip of coffee and then looked them over one by one. 'I'm thinking of crossing the river ourselves. Lyle Colbert has ten, a dozen men in his camp, doesn't he? How many are guarding the chain where it's moored across the river?'

'Usually two, sometimes three,' Lofton answered.

'That makes it an easier target, does it not?' Ned asked. 'If we can slip across the river and take care of the guards, we should be able to unfasten the chain over there.'

'Sure!' Andy said with excitement. 'We can handle the guards, take the tree down and slip the chain before anyone from this side of the river could reach us.'

'I don't know,' Mack Paulsen said, wagging his head heavily. 'It's a good enough plan as far as it goes. I've considered it before, but it invites retaliation, doesn't it? All-out war. All Colbert would have to do is grapple the chain out of the river and reattach it. Meanwhile, he'll be mad as hell and likely he'll send gunmen after us to settle things.'

'It would give us all enough time to get our timber to the sawmill,' Andy said, still excited by the prospect of action after months of sitting idly.

'Sure,' Paulsen said unhappily. 'And after that, assuming we lived through the attempt, what then?'

'We'd be right back where we started,' Lofton agreed, 'but probably with a fewer timbermen.'

'You could hire more,' Andy said, still flooded with ambition.

'Not unless we paid fighting wages. The word'll get around.'

'That's true,' Orson Bright said as Mother Rose filled his coffee cup again. 'What else can we do?'

'Nothing,' Ned Browning said, rising from the table. 'Just like you have been doing for months. Don't do anything. Sit here until you're broke and hungry and driven off your land, whipped like dogs. I don't care! Do what you like. If you're not willing to fight for what you have, you just might as well pack up now and pull out.'

Having spoken, Ned strode to the door, flung it open and stepped out into the clear light of morning. He liked none of this. What was he doing now, trying to spur men into a gunfight? What he had said was true enough, but what gave him the right to condemn other men to death?

He walked slowly through the trees. The smoke from the chimney dissipated almost as soon as it puffed from the chimney in the breeze that was shuffling the tall trees. The river glinted silver-blue before him. He walked that way and found Tess seated on a low rock, her arms looped around her knees, staring out at the flowing river. He said nothing, but she must have sensed him or seen his shadow, because she turned and glanced up, not quite smiling, not quite frowning.

'What are they talking about back there?' she asked.

'I don't know. They asked for my two-cents' worth and I gave it to them.'

'You urged them to fight?'

'What else could I tell them? It's their only chance. Fight or pull up stakes and move on.'

'They're not gunfighters. Just hardworking timbermen,' Tess said, returning her gaze to the quick-flowing river.

'I know that.'

'Anyway, what's so bad about pulling out? Starting over in a better place?'

'Nothing, maybe. Maybe that's what I should do – if I knew of a better place.'

They were silent for a time, listening to the forest sounds, the rustling of the tree branches, a dislodged pinecone falling to earth, the squawk of jaybirds and the chattering of squirrels. Beyond all that was the river endlessly rolling away.

'You are the first one Lyle Colbert will want to take care of, Ned,' Tess finally commented. 'The rest of them, Father included, have taken it for so long that Colbert knows they will not stand up and fight now. They'll buckle under . . . if you are not around.'

'What are you saying?' Ned asked, drawing nearer to the blond-haired girl.

'I'm saying,' her eyes were over-bright as she rose and turned to face him. She took both of his hands in her smaller ones. 'If *you* were to pull out, Ned, the others would lose heart. And you would be away to a safer place.'

'Then what would you think of me?' Ned asked carefully.

'Then I'd think that you were alive out there somewhere!' Her voice lowered, 'And possibly thinking of me on some lonely evening.'

He kissed her.

She drew away, not really surprised but vaguely discomfited. Did that mean that he was going to do as she requested or that he must stay on so that her respect of him was in no way diminished? She would have spoken to ask, but at that moment Mother Rose appeared on the trail, carrying two empty buckets on a yoke across her bird-thin shoulders.

'You forgot the water buckets this morning,' Mother Rose said to Tess. 'I don't know where your mind is these days.' But she did. Mother

Rose was old, but that did not mean that she had no memory of what could spring up in a young girl's heart, sometimes without warning of any kind.

'You can go along,' Mother Rose said to Ned. 'I'll help the girl. The men have reached a decision.'

Ned Browning nodded, let his eyes meet Tess's again briefly before she turned sharply away toward the river, buckets in hand. He realized that he had disappointed her, that he had not responded directly to her request. How could he have? He had an obligation to Orson Bright.

He had taken Bright's money, money he could not readily spare, in return for a promise to help the old man fight for his land. A man can't just walk away from his obligations. You lived up to your word, and that was that. Or you were not a man. Gloomily, a little angrily, Ned strode on up the forest path, returning to the cabin.

Lyle Colbert sat behind the dark oak desk in his office. Sunlight glinted blue on the window. Colbert was as pale and bloodless as a wax figure. His eyes, flanking a hooked nose, were as bright as sapphires. His hands were white, tapering, his fingernails too long for a man's. He was very rich and at this time of life he wanted only one thing – to become richer. Observing Lyle Colbert and his austere habits, his lack of humor, one would have been inclined to almost pity his dreary, soulless life, but Colbert himself was quite pleased with his narrow existence. He had virtually no knowledge of life beyond a dedication to amassing gold. He had no heirs, no one to bequeath his wealth to, but that had no relevance to him. He would have it while he was here, and have it he did. By the bushel. It was enough satisfaction to him. He needed nothing else. Let lesser men worry about trivialities. The door to his office opened a few inches and a shy voice announced:

'He's here, Mr Colbert.'

'All right,' Lyle Colbert replied to his secretary. 'Bring him in.'

After a minute the door opened again, wider this time and a dark-eyed man with a flourishing black mustache entered. He had his hat on his head. The light picked out the silver conchos on his belt. He wore his ivory-handled Colt low on his hip. He crossed the room, started to perch on the corner of Colbert's desk, reconsidered, and stood facing Lyle Colbert with a white-toothed grin.

'Good morning, Santana,' Lyle Colbert said. 'I'm happy to see you again.'

SIX

'I wasn't sure if you would get my message,' Lyle Colbert was saying. He had not risen to his feet to welcome the gunfighter, nor had he offered Santana a chair. The line had to be drawn between employer and employee.

'Here I am,' Santana said, flashing another of his smiles. 'What's happening, Mr Colbert? Don't tell me that Bright's other pup thinks he's grown up enough now to handle their affairs.'

'Andy Bright is involved,' Colbert said. 'But he is not much of a problem.' Colbert hesitated, examining his pale hands. 'The fellow he is riding with might be. He shot down Royce Traylor.'

Santana was no longer smiling. Royce Traylor had been good with a gun, very good. Not as good as Santana believed himself to be, but good.

'Was it a fair fight?' he asked.

'From all reports.' Lyle Colbert seemed to be holding something back. Now he proceeded: 'They say that it was Frank Lavender who did the shooting.'

'Lavender?' Santana was momentarily stuck for a reply. He had once ridden with Frank Lavender. The man was lightning quick with a gun. 'Who says it was Lavender?'

'That's the name he was using.'

Santana was thoughtful. 'I thought I'd heard that they had him locked up in the Cheyenne jail, fitting him for a rope necktie.'

'Maybe he broke out,' Colbert said.

'Why in hell would he be fighting for a penny-ante outfit like the Brights?'

'They say that Frank took a liking to Bright's daughter. Do you remember her?'

Santana nodded. Tess Bright was too young for him, but there was no denying that she was a cute little thing. Still, hiring out your gun for the sake of a woman seemed a fool's bargain and Frank Lavender was no fool.

'There has to be more to it,' Santana said.

'Possibly, but that's beside the point, isn't it? They tell me that Lavender is a dead shot, and a quick one,' Colbert said, tilting back in his chair to let his eyes meet Santana's directly. 'Can you take him?' he asked the gunfighter.

'For a price, even if it is Frank Lavender,' Santana answered. 'If I can't take him quick, I'll take him sure.'

'Like the other Bright kid?' Colbert said, needling Santana.

'I just did that because the kid's bragging was annoying me. I just happened to see him passing that alley.'

'Most everyone seemed to believe that story about you and Dan Bright, about you and he having a fight over that woman . . . what was her name?'

'Doris,' Santana said sourly. He would never have lowered himself far enough to fall for a tramp like that, but the story was widely accepted.

'Where is she now?' Colbert asked.

'I gave her a few dollars and a stage ticket to Bainbridge. I didn't want her getting drunk or careless and changing her story.'

'Very good,' Lyle Colbert replied. 'You are a thinking man, Santana. It's what puts you a notch or two ahead of these other would-be gunfighters. Very well,' he said decisively. 'I'll pay you double what you got for Dan Bright. Just make sure you eliminate Frank Lavender.'

Frank Lavender was sitting in the canoe as Billy Lofton and Mack Paulson paddled it across the Snake River on that day. Andy Bright was along as well. His father had objected, saying that he needed him at home in case Lyle Colbert decided to storm their landhold. 'Then send for Shockley and Bert Smart,' had been Andy's response to his father's concern. Young Andy Bright was determined to get into some sort of action against Colbert.

'Besides,' Andy went on, 'we should be back before Colbert can get his men organized.'

'If you make it back,' Orson said, worry lining his face. He had lost one son to Colbert's gang. He did not intend to lose another.

'Frank'll take care of me,' Andy said confidently. He flickered a glance toward Ned Browning who stood waiting, rifle in hand. He made no response. When the bullets start to fly no man can be certain he can protect another.

Tess sat on the front porch, elbows on her knees, chin cupped in her hands as she watched the four men tramp off toward the river and the waiting canoe. She said nothing. She had already spoken to Ned, told him how she felt about the fighting. He would not listen, either out of a sense of obligation to her father or because of his own foolish notion of manhood. She would wait, do what she always did at such times: curse men for the fools they were and pray that they would return safely.

Through the dark ranks of the pines they could clearly see two Colbert men. Was that all there were? There was no way of knowing. These two seemed to be pretty nonchalant about their guard duties. Likely they had hired on as fighting men and the idea of being posted to guard a tree did nothing to excite them. One man, the one in the blue silk shirt, sat on a flat rock, his Winchester rifle beside him, the other, who was talking just now, was leaning against the great tree where the chain was fixed. If he had a rifle it was not evident, but he wore his twin Colts as if he knew what they were for.

Ned Browning glanced at his party. Andy Bright was nearly beside him, stretching his neck forward like a dog waiting to be loosed from its leash, pistol in hand. A few yards back Billy

Lofton and Mack Paulsten crouched, their faces anxious. Farther back along the trail, Ned knew were three lumberjacks. Two of them carrying a twelve-foot-long timber saw, the other a double-bitted axe.

Ned nodded to Andy and they slipped to where Paulsen and Lofton waited uneasily. Ned whispered to them: 'We're going to try to do this as quietly as possible. There's no telling how shots will carry across the river, and we don't want Colbert's gang alerted.'

'You have a plan?' Paulsen asked. His voice was thin and high with tension.

'Not much of one,' Ned had to admit. 'But it's worth a try. Andy, you cover me from the trees – but for God's sake don't shoot unless it's absolutely necessary.'

Andy nodded silent agreement. Taking a deep breath then, adjusting his face into a smile, Ned Browning turned and walked boldly toward the outlaws.

'Hey, Riley!' the man who had been talking said urgently and the outlaw on the rock snatched up his Winchester and leaped to his feet as Ned Browning entered the clearing where the two stood watch.

'Good morning, gents,' Ned said.

'Who the hell are you and what are you doing here?' the man with the twin Colts demanded.

'Take it easy, friend!' Ned said, still smiling. 'I'm a man afoot, trying to find a way to ford the river. I'm trying to reach Hoyt's Camp. Is everyone around here so unfriendly?'

'Just keep moving,' the gunman suggested, his hands on the butts of his pistols.

'I told you, I'm trying a way to do just that,' Ned said agreeably. 'I'm just trying to find a way to ford the river.'

'How was you planning on doing it in the first place?' the man with the rifle asked.

'I'm afoot now, as I told you. My horse broke a leg. Originally, I was figuring on riding it across. Old Patches was a strong swimmer. Once down along the Milk River—'

'We don't need to hear no old war stories,' the man with the Winchester, Riley, said. 'We told you to keep moving. Do it.'

Ned had eased nearer as he spoke, still smiling stupidly. Now he shrugged, using only his hands and began to turn away. He launched himself then at the man with the two revolvers, gripping both of the Colbert man's wrists. He smashed his skull into the gunman's nose, feeling the hot spurt of blood as bone cracked. The rifleman, Riley, had started to raise his Winchester, but realized that he was too close to fire. Any bullet that missed by inches, even one that tagged Ned, was likely to hit his partner.

The man with two guns sagged in Ned's hands. And knowing he could not hold him up any longer, he released him, lunged at the rifleman and managed to get both hands on the barrel of the Winchester as Riley back-pedaled away. Riley's eyes were wide with fear. The barrel of his rifle was now aimed at the treetops and Ned Browning was the stronger man.

The pistol boomed behind Ned. Gunsmoke drifted across the clearing as Riley's hands fell away from the rifle. The gunman slumped to the earth, his hands clawing at air. Ned hurled the captured rifle away and spun angrily to see Andy Bright, flushed with triumph, emerge from the trees.

'I got him!' Andy said excitedly. Ned didn't speak a word. As Lofton and Paulsen entered the clearing, Ned Browning was crouched down over the two-gun man, disarming him.

'Help me tie this one up,' Ned said to Paulsen.

'I got the other one with a clean shot,' Andy was babbling.

'I told you not to shoot,' Ned growled without rising to face Andy.

'There wasn't any choice,' Andy said, holstering his weapon.

'Looked to me like the situation was well in hand,' Billy Lofton said sourly.

'That shot might have been heard across the river,' Paulsen said to his friend. 'They might think it meant something, might not. All the same, get the boys working on this tree now!'

After binding the gunman with his own belt and bandana, Ned stood, hands on his hips, studying the opposite bank of the river. Behind him the three-man crew of lumberjacks had begun their work. The man with the axe was cutting a notch in the tree, ensuring that the tree fell away from the river as those with the two-man saw began working on the opposite side of the big pine.

'Think they could have heard it?' Ned asked as Mack Paulsen eased up beside hint

'There's no telling. I've heard hunters on the opposite side from time to time – it all depends.'

'It was just one shot!' Andy Bright was

protesting. 'That could signify anything!'

'Anything at all,' Ned agreed, now facing young Andy Bright for the first time. 'But if you're wary, ready for an attack like Lyle Colbert's crew is, it could alert them, suggest that maybe they should take a look to see what the shot did signify.'

There was nothing they could do about it now. They continued to watch the opposite shore for any gathering of men, for a boat being launched from Colbert's stronghold. Meanwhile, the saw continued to bite deeply into the pale wood of the big pine. The two lumbermen were strong, used to this work and competent, but still five feet of green wood was going to take some time to cut through.

'Billy,' Mack Paulsen said to his friend, 'why don't you go back upstream? Your crews and mine should be ready to launch the barges at a moment's notice. You'll be able to see the pine when its felled, it'll riffle the rest of the trees around when it goes. Raise anchor then, and start downriver. We'll be only seconds getting the chain off the stump. My crew, tell Lew he's to take my barge with you. If I can't catch up, well, he's in charge.'

'Andy,' Ned Browning said. 'You'd better get across the river, if Billy will loan you his canoe. Get to your father and tell him what the plan is. Have Amos and Bert Smart ready to start the timber barges downriver at the first sign that Billy's and Mack's crews are heading that way. Three barges together, each with armed men on board, will have a better chance of making it.'

'But you—' Andy began to object. Ned cut him off.

'Get back there. And tell Mother Rose and Tess they're to go with you. They can't stay behind, not with the mood Lyle Colbert's going to be in. Now get going!'

Ned returned to where Billy Lofton stood watching the river. The man they had tied up glared up ferociously at Ned Browning as he passed. The Colbert man was struggling with his bonds, trying to curse past the gag in his mouth. 'Just take it easy,' Ned told him, 'your friends are bound to come looking for you sooner or later.'

'Looks like sooner, Frank,' Billy Lofton said. He raised an arm to indicate the far bank of the river with a pointing finger. 'Someone's launching a boat. Either they heard the shot or it's time to relieve these two guards. Either way,' Lofton said anxiously, 'we don't have much time.'

The rowboat, painted blue and white, carried only three men. Two of these were at the oars. Rowing across the river was not easy. They had to angle into the current upstream to keep from being swept away. Nevertheless, these two seemed to have had some practice at their job. The boat neared slowly but inexorably as the lumbermen sawed frantically at the bulky pine tree. Glancing at the trunk of the tree, Ned could see that they were still no more than halfway through.

'Looks like we're going to have to hold them back,' Lofton said.

'No,' Ned said. He now held Riley's Winchester in his hand. 'Just me. You'd be helping more if you go back to the timber camp and assist Mack. I'll send your 'jacks on the run once the tree is felled.'

'Even if you manage to hold them off,' Billy said, studying the blue and white boat, 'More shooting will alert Colbert to what's really going on.'

'Yes, it will.' Ned's mouth tightened. 'We all knew it from the start. Maybe we'd hoped it would be different, but it won't be: you'll have to fight your way downriver.'

95

Ned watched the approaching boat with narrowed eyes, glancing only now and then at the slow progress of the lumberjacks. The men were bathed in sweat, strain showing on their faces. They were used to this kind of work, but seldom had they had this sort of pressure to contend with.

The boat was near enough now so that Ned could make out the faces of the approaching men. He considered firing a warning shot, but that would only alert them to trouble sooner. In another few minutes there would be no choice. The tree had to be felled; the chain had to be raised. That was all there was to it. The entire plan rested on that; the livelihoods of all of the timbermen depended on it. The man in the bow of the boat was standing now, and Ned quite distinctly saw him raise a pointing finger in their direction.

'Get back!' one of the 'jacks shouted urgently and Ned frowned at the man, not understanding. 'Get away!' the timberhand shouted again.

Ned leaped aside as the great tree shivered and groaned. Then it toppled with an explosion like muted cannon fire. Ned, who had expected it to fall in near silence, stared with amazement. As the huge pine fell, the lower end of the tree kicked back toward where the men with the saw and Ned had been standing. Had he not been warned, Ned would have been battered by the tons of timber.

The treetop smashed into the surrounding trees, sending tremors through the ranks of pines. The trunk began to roll off of the stump and slowly settle to the ground. Branches had flown like shrapnel, the dust cloud around them was thick and roiling.

That signaled the watching men in the boat and immediately rifles aimed at their position opened fire. 'Run for it, men!' Ned ordered. 'I'll take care of the chain. No, leave that saw, just go!'

There was no argument. The timbermen took to their heels, disappearing through the forest. Ned went to one knee and fired three carefully spaced shots through the barrel of his Winchester, sending the boatmen to the sheltering bottom of their craft. There was a brief lull then and Ned used it to return to the jagged stump of the pine. Placing his rifle aside, he gripped the heavy chain with both hands and pulled. The massive steel links moved no more than six inches and then could be lifted no farther. Ned cursed himself for having let the lumberjacks run away so soon. It was obvious that it would take two men, one on either side of the stump, to alternately lift the steel collar.

He did not have two men. Holding the section of chain he had lifted as high as possible, he eased his way to the far side of the stump and lifted the section there. Then he shifted back to the other side. It was slow going. The two-inch links of chain were even heavier than he had imagined them to be.

And now the riflemen in the boat had opened up again. They were still too far out for clean shots, but the hum and thwack of their bullets moving past his head to clip branches from the surrounding trees was near enough to unnerve him. He worked on frantically, his own shirt now soaked with perspiration.

Inch by inch he raised the chain, alternating sides of the stump. Glancing across his shoulder, he could see the blue and white boat, ever nearer. A trio of shots sounded, their reports nearer at hand, and one of the bullets – a lucky shot? – tagged the huge stump of the tree only inches from his hand, near enough to send bark flying into his face with stinging force.

Only a little more. He repeated this to himself as he continued to labor, cursing wildly when he lost his grip and the chain slid down a few inches. Only a little more. Eyeing the boat he saw that the oarsmen were making much better progress at their chore than he was. The temptation was to drop the chain, snatch up his rifle and give them a taste of their own medicine, but that would gain him nothing. The chain would slither its way back to the roots and he would have to begin all over again. He let the bullets whip past, although he worked now in a crouch . . . as if that would do much good.

Only a little more. He had worked a few links of the chain up onto the newly cut white meat of the stump, and he fought to hold them there, his shoulders trembling, his eyes stinging with perspiration. He could not let the chain go now. Carefully, with one hand securing those links, he worked back around to the far side of the tree, lifting, straining to bring the chain up one link at a time.

It was free! One half of the girdling chain lay like a defeated silver snake across the jagged stump. Ned left it there for the moment. Leaping toward his Winchester he shouldered it and emptied the magazine in the direction of the boat, sending the men aboard diving under the thwarts again.

Throwing away the empty rifle, Ned hefted the massive chain in both arms, and while the men cowered in their boat, he hobbled to the edge of the river and dropped the chain into the water. He did not throw it, no man could have, but it was free and the current would drift it inexorably away from shore. A man rose up from the bottom of the boat and another shot was loosed in his direction.

Ned drew his Colt and returned the shot only to warn the men that he still had teeth, then he struck out through the forest. There was no triumphant exhilaration in his chest, only the hot pain of exertion. If the others thought that they had just won a victory, Ned Browning knew that they had just begun a war.

SEVEN

Weaving through the timber at a dead run, Ned Browning burst into the timber camp, startling the three lumberjacks who stood there, drinking water from tin cups. Unnerved at first, the three now recognized Ned and, smiling, they gathered around him.

'You cut that close,' one of them, the man who had wielded the axe said, clapping Ned's shoulder.

'Too close,' Ned agreed. He was standing half-bent over, struggling to regain his breath. 'But the chain's in the river. When are Lofton and Paulson starting downriver?'

'Any minute now. You'll hear a whistle blow. Are you going with them?'

'No,' Ned replied. 'How about you boys?'

'We thought of it, but we decided to go into the high timber. We've got a shack up there. No one is likely to find us, and if they do, they'll be sorry.'

'You say you're not going on the barges either?' one of them asked Ned, handing him a cup of water.

'No. I need to get back across the river. Is there another canoe that I can use?'

'There is. A couple of them. Have you much experience with canoes?'

'None,' Ned admitted, handing the tin cup back. The three smiled tolerantly.

'You won't make it alone, then. Not with that current. Thomas? What do you say that you and I take the man across the river?'

'Sure. He saved our bacon, didn't he? Just wait until after the barges have started, mister. We wouldn't want to get in front of one of those. They don't stop.'

Ned agreed and expressed his thanks. He stood then on the riverbank, watching the Snake flow. A piercing whistle sounded minutes later and, glancing upstream, he could see the heavily laden timber barges begin to drift from the shore and catch the swift current. They glided, these bulky monsters, on the silver face of the big river. As they floated nearer, Ned could see that each of these two barges carried half a dozen riflemen hidden behind or among the massive trunks of the timber.

From the corner of his eye he saw other movement and, glancing that way . . . across the river . . . he saw that Orson Bright had launched his timber barge as well. He waited, watching as the first barge disappeared around the bend in the river. Riflemen began to fire from across the river, from Lyle Colbert's camp, and the boatmen answered. He doubted if anyone could hit anyone else under these conditions, still enough guns were being fired so that their smoke gathered in dark wreaths across the surface of the river.

Bright's barge was now nearly abreast of where Ned stood watching. Bright was at the tiller, sheltered by two huge logs which had been positioned that far back to afford cover for him. Behind the logs, Amos Shockley and Bert Smart could be seen. Andy Bright had clambered up onto the stack of timber to be able to shoot better.

Where was Tess!

There was no sign of the girl nor of Mother Rose. Damn Andy! He had been told to make sure that Tess and Mother Rose were on the barge. There was no sign of the women, and Ned would have seen them if they were on board, since they would be riding on the sheltered side of the boat.

Farther along, the guns continued to roar. Lyle Colbert's men had not given up yet. Colbert himself must have known that he was beaten for the moment. But it would be a short-lived victory. As had been pointed out, Colbert would simply order the chain grappled from the river depths and reattached on the south bank.

Perhaps a moral victory was better than none; maybe the timbermen would be emboldened enough to fight for themselves once they had delivered their logs to the sawmill.

'You ready to go?' the lumberjack named Thomas asked. At Ned's nod, he said. 'Good, the boys and me are wanting to get up in the tall timber as quick as possible in case Colbert takes a notion to burn out the camps while Lofton and Paulsen are gone.'

A canoe was dragged from the trees and held for Ned. Stepping in, the two timbermen shoved off into the swift current, one of them nimbly boarding from the water to take a kneeling position at the bow, the other similarly positioned behind Ned.

They had been right. There was no way Ned Browning could have crossed this river alone in a canoe. These two were skilled at battling the current, and sure in their paddle strokes. The light craft skimmed rapidly across the rolling river to the far shore where Ned clambered out, shouted his thanks, waved a hand and entered the deep woods below the Bright cabin.

The shadows were deep and cool, the long ranks of the trees nearly blue. Jays and an occasional woodpecker whirred away at his approach, but there was no other movement, no other sound in the deep forest.

No smoke rose from the stone chimney of the cabin. No one called out as he reached the yard, crossed it, and mounted the front porch. The door stood closed; the latch string was out. Ned felt his heart sink a little. The house *felt* empty. He knew before he toed the door open and entered, pistol in his hand, that he would find no one there.

Tess Bright stood at the door of the timberline shack where Amos Shockley and Bert Smart lived. Mother Rose lay behind her on Bert's cot, her narrow chest rising and falling shallowly. She was not sick, she had told them, only tired.

When Andy Bright had burst into the house, his eyes excited, his words wildly spoken, he had given his command: 'You two have to get over to the barge mooring. We're going downriver to the sawmill. Now! Frank Lavender says to make sure that you're on board, Tess.'

'I'm not going,' Mother Rose said, keeping her back to them as she scraped the top of her stove. 'I'm too old to jump on a raft and ride the river with men shooting. You go if you must, Tess.'

Tess stood irresolutely between her brother and her grandmother. 'You've got to hurry,' Andy went on as if Mother Rose had said nothing. 'The barge will be off in a matter of minutes.'

'Why does Ned say I should go?' Tess managed to ask.

'Ned? Oh, *Frank*! He's afraid that the Colbert bunch might take a notion to ride over here and burn down the place. And who knows what else.'

'We won't be losing much,' Mother Rose said in a dry, far-away voice.

'We should go,' Tess tried.

'No.' The old woman's voice was thin but firm. 'I'm riding no riverboat.'

Tess looked at Andy as if to say, 'You see how it is.' Shaking her head, she told her brother: 'I guess I'll be staying too.' It wouldn't do to let Mother Rose stay alone. Maybe she could at least talk the old woman into slipping away to a safer place.

And so they had trudged up along the mountain trail to the tiny shack where Shockley and Bert sheltered. Mother Rose had almost immediately stretched out on Bert's poor cot, claiming that she was not used to such exertions – mountain climbing was nearly as bad as river-rafting. It seemed to Tess, however, that there was more to Mother Rose's complaint than she was willing to share.

Now Tess stood at the leather-hinged door to the shack, looking downslope toward their cabin in the pines. She could barely make out the chimney and a portion of the roof, but she would have seen anyone approaching up the road. The timber barges were gone around the river bend. They had begun their journey to the sawmill while she and Mother Rose were still in the forest, climbing toward the lumberjack's shack. It was strange to see no one anywhere, no sign of life. Nothing but the long blue-green ranks of trees in

107

whichever direction she looked – that and the silver glint of the Snake River making its way south toward Hoyt's Camp and the faraway places.

Tess's heart suddenly jumped. For riding along the road now, not toward them but away, she saw the buckskin horse well enough. It was Andy's. And riding it was a man with a blue shirt much like the one Ned Browning had been wearing. There was no point in shouting; she would not be heard. No point in waving; she would not be seen, and so she simply watched as Ned rode down the mountain, feeling her heart ride with him.

Ned Browning had searched the empty cabin and then walked out into the bright sunlight to ponder. Where had the women gone? Had they been aboard the timber barge after all, concealed somehow so that he had missed seeing them? Andy had been told to make sure that the women were on board. Orson would not have left them behind if they were in danger. No, they were safe. The question was, what should he, himself, do now?

He was not going to wait idly at the cabin with all of the activity that was certainly taking place downriver. He considered matters and decided that he might be of use at Hoyt's Camp. It seemed possible that Lyle Colbert would send some men to disrupt matters at the sawmill. Furious at having the timbermen defeat his river chain, he might see a chance of denying them success if his riders could get there overland ahead of the barges.

It was far from certain that Colbert would attempt any such drastic step, since as everyone knew, the barges would not be making a second trip and the timbermen would find themselves back in the same position as they were previously. Still, Ned did not know Colbert, did not know how the man's mind worked. He might take the practical route and simply use patience to defeat the loggers, or he might be the sort to retaliate in a fury at the revenue he had been deprived of. There was no way of knowing. Ned decided to be on hand when Colbert made his intentions clear. If he could reach Hoyt's Camp soon enough.

In the lean-to stable behind the cabin, Ned found Andy Bright's buckskin horse and Orson's shaggy gray. That animal looked to be nearly Orson's age. It eyed Ned morosely as it champed on a twist of hay. Reaching for Andy's saddle, Ned rigged up the younger horse and started down the mountain toward the town of Hoyt's Camp.

The forest depths were cool, the sun a flickering apparition behind the ranks of pines. Only here and there when the forest thinned did golden rays of light strike the dark earth. The road was a winding corridor through primeval time.

Or so it seemed until the mounted men emerged from the trees on either side of the road, flanking Ned Browning's way.

There were five of them. Their leader seemed to be a man riding a paint pony. He wore a wide-brimmed black hat, white shirt, a belt studded with silver conchos. He had a dark, sharp-featured face and a narrow mustache.

'Who are you and where are you going?' he asked Ned.

'What's all of this?' Ned asked, feigning complete surprise. He knew full well who they must be, but none of them could know him. The man from the barroom fight was not among them.

'You will answer,' the Spanish-looking man said coldly.

'Sure. I'm Ned Browning. Just a traveling man,

heading for Hoyt's Camp. I heard there might be work there.'

'A traveling man ... a saddle tramp, you mean?' the leader of the gang asked.

Ned shrugged and grinned sheepishly. 'If you care to put it that way,' he answered.

'He's riding from the Bright property,' one of the other riders, a red-faced man with jug-handle ears said with a scowl.

'What are you doing up here?' their leader asked in a soft voice.

'Saw a cabin. Figured I might get some grub,' Ned said. 'Like I say, I'm just dragging the line and a meal is hard to come by. But there was no one home.'

'I don't believe him,' the red-faced man said sourly. 'Let's put him out of his misery.'

Santana, for that was who their leader was, shook his head negatively, emphatically. No, they would not kill a man they did not even know. Santana did not approve of indiscriminate killing. He had once ridden with a man called 'Wild Bill' Buckley who had killed sixteen men that Santana knew of. One night Buckley had gotten himself drunk and senselessly shot down a fanner whose looks he didn't care for. That was the one that they hanged 'Wild Bill' for. When Santana killed it was not on a whim; killing was a business.

'No,' Santana said calmly. 'We have other work to attend to.' He turned his attention back to Ned. 'If I were you, traveling man, I would find myself a meal in Hoyt's Camp and then travel on. This is going to be bad country to be in for a long time.'

Ned said nothing. The riders rode past him, the red-faced man's horse brushing against the flank of Ned's buckskin. He turned in the saddle to watch them ride away. He was not so concerned with what they might do now that he knew that Tess was not at home. There wasn't much he could have done to stop five armed men anyway. He started the buckskin down through the long stand on pines toward Hoyt's Camp.

The sawmill stood on the river bank where the elbow bend ended and the Snake began to widen and slow as it spread out across the land. Here, there was still a stiff current to turn the massive wooden waterwheel which powered the saw. Just now the first of the three barges was unloading its timber and the mule skinners whose animals would be used to tow the empty barges back upstream were dickering with the boatmen. The sawmill owner was directing his men, counting board feet and estimating his profit.

Lyle Colbert sat in his surrey, watching the activity with narrowed eyes. He was estimating how much revenue he had lost and calculating how much more he would charge the loggers for their next passage once the chain was again fixed in place and guarded by a substantially larger crew. They hadn't beaten him, and they must know that as well. All they had accomplished was to spit in his eye. Lyle Colbert wasn't the sort to forgive.

By now, Santana should have reached the Bright house and the men in the boats he had sent across the river would have begun re-affixing the chain before they stormed the homes belonging to Lofton and Mack Paulsen. The loggers would not have a happy homecoming.

The timbermen had shot their wad. They could have this brief moment of satisfaction, but that was all they were to gain by their recklessness. The river belonged to one man – Lyle Colbert – and he would reclaim it. He would not strangle the life from the timber camps, for he needed that revenue, but he would make sure that no man from the upriver camps again had the audacity to challenge his authority.

If a few of the loggers had to die before his point was made, well, so be it.

Santana's men had searched the Bright house, finding it empty. Combing the nearby woods they found no one. The property was unguarded. The red-faced man, the one named Jeter stamped from the house to face Santana who sat his paint horse, surveying the countryside.

'Nothing, no one,' Jeter said. 'Want me to torch it?'

'No,' Santana said. 'Not yet.'

'That's what Mr Colbert wants,' Jeter complained sulkily. Santana did not like this one. He was too anxious to kill, to destroy, too lazy to think ahead.

'I am aware of what Mr Colbert wants,' Santana said in a chilly voice. 'It is not yet time for it.'

'I don't know what in hell you mean,' Jeter said in exasperation.

'Of course you don't,' Santana replied disparagingly. 'I will explain, although I owe you no explanation. I have been hired to find and eliminate Frank Lavender. Obviously he is not here. Probably he went down the river on one of the barges. Eventually he will return to this house, but if it is burned to the ground, there will be nothing for him to return to. Do you understand? I intend to wait here for the return of Frank Lavender. After I have killed him, then I will burn down the house with him in it.'

EIGHT

Andy Bright was half-full of whiskey when Ned Browning located him in the saloon. Ned's mouth tightened and he strode across the plank floor of the place to the bar where Andy Bright stood, his elbows hooked on the scarred surface of the bar. A few apparently bored fellow drinkers were listening to Andy's tale of the running gunfight on the trip downriver. Men glanced at Ned, but no one reacted to his presence.

'Where's Tess?' Ned demanded without any preliminaries.

'Frank! How are you, Frank?' Andy said expansively.

'Where's your sister?' Ned asked roughly.

'At home,' Andy replied with a few drunken blinks.

'No, she isn't. I just came from there. I told you to make sure that she went along with the barges.'

'Not home?' Andy said blankly. ''S funny. She said she was going to stay there. Mother Rose refused to come along, so Tess decided to stay with her.' Andy's mood shifted as Ned continued to glower at him. 'What was I supposed to do, hog tie her!'

'Never mind,' Ned said, not to placate Andy, but because he knew that he was going to get no further information from the drunken timberman. Tess was still on the mountain, had to be, but somehow he had missed her. 'Andy, I've got your horse.'

'Keep it,' Andy said, waving his hand at Ned. 'I'm going to buy me a new one anyway. It's payday, you know, thanks to you.'

Ned Browning didn't respond. There was no point in talking to someone as drunk as Andy Bright was just then. Andy, on the other hand, was feeling garrulous. He continued talking, loudly enough for everyone in the saloon to hear him.

'As soon as my Dad gets his money from the timber we're going to hire us some men, and they won't all be lumberjacks, either! They'll be fighting men. Lyle Colbert doesn't know what

117

kind of a fight he's in for.'

When Ned pushed his way out through the green door into the open air, Andy was still regaling the men in the saloon. They were standing for it, apparently, because Andy was setting up drinks all around. Ned wondered idly what Orson Bright would think of this. Not only was Andy drunk, spending much money, but he had more or less challenged Lyle Colbert in public.

He gave it no more thought. Riding to the sawmill, he encountered Mack Paulsen and Billy Lofton who were watching the barges be unloaded. He inquired about Tess.

'No, Frank, she never did come downriver. We thought maybe she was with you,' big Mack Paulsen said, concern showing in his eyes.

'I couldn't find her. Where's Orson?'

'In the mill office.'

'If you see him,' Ned said, 'warn him that there's some of Colbert riders up near his house. I imagine they've sent some men up to your places too.'

'We've all been kind of expecting that,' Lofton said. 'We're looking to recruit some help before we start back up the mountain.'

Ned didn't know how much help men hired off the street would be in a fight with Lyle Colbert's professional gunmen, but he said nothing. His only concern now was Tess's safety.

He started the weary buckskin horse back toward the tall timber. He rode warily now, knowing that Colbert's soldiers were around. He had gotten away with a lie the first time he had encountered them. There was no way they would believe him again.

The day was growing cool, the breeze freshening, swaying the ranks of tall trees. The sun, lowering now, was filtered to near darkness by the pines. He had ridden two or three miles, turning the question this way and that before a notion occurred to him, and when it did, he wondered at his own stupidity for not having thought of it before.

Tess had been warned that the Colbert riders might be headed for their property. She was a smart girl, and if she could not run, because of Mother Rose, she would have found a place to hide. Where? The answer now seemed fairly obvious.

Amos Shockley and Bert Smart lived in a shack deep in the timber. Ned had never seen it, but

119

Tess certainly knew where it was located. No outsiders sent to the Bright place would be likely to guess where the shack was. With increasing hope and growing concern, Ned Browning urged the buckskin horse on. The day was growing cooler, darker. A deepening gloom settled across the land.

Santana had sent his band of men back to Colbert's stronghold. They were of no use waiting around the Bright place. They could be better utilized elsewhere. Their assigned task was different from Santana's own. He had been hired to do one job, and he intended to fulfill his contract to kill Frank Lavender. And if what everyone had told him was correct, Lavender would not leave Tess Bright. They would be back, and Santana would be there waiting when they did come.

Santana walked out of the shadowed house into the yard where he watched the sun dropping slowly toward the western horizon above the dark ranks of trees. The Snake River itself was dark in this light, only here and there glinting silver where a stray shaft of sun touched its surface.

Turning in a slow circle, Santana surveyed the

land around him. It was a rugged, heavily forested land. Inhospitable, if highly profitable for those who dared to challenge it. He wondered. . . .

And then he saw it. Santana's body stiffened, he squinted, watching the sky intently, and slowly he let a smile part his lips. There was a thin wisp of smoke rising from somewhere along the forest flank. Wind-whipped, it did not rise high or remain for long. It was bent by the breeze and then quickly dissipated by it. But it was there, quite definitely there. Santana walked to where he had left his horse tied, whistling as he went.

Tess knew she should not have started the fire in the iron stove. But Mother Rose was deathly sick. The old woman had protested that she was not ill, but her condition became undeniable as they sheltered in the shack, waiting for the men to return. Mother Rose had begun to tremble, and after placing all the blankets Tess could find over her, she still shivered. Her face was nearly blue, and night was going to settle soon, bringing the chill of the high mountains with it.

In the end, casting caution aside, Tess had started a fire in the stove, more concerned with

Mother Rose's life than that some raiding party might see the smoke rising from the iron pipe. She sat now beside Mother Rose's bed, holding the old woman's cold, bony hand. She watched the red and gold of the low flames behind the grate of the potbelly stove, realizing that the warmth it was casting off might not be enough to keep away the long, long chill hovering near Mother Rose.

The day grew darker, the night birds began to chitter, sounding as if they were shivering in the cool of evening. An owl hooted – only once – and far, far away a timber wolf raised a mournful howl to the skies.

The door to the shack was kicked open and the room was flooded with cold air. Spinning around, Tess rose to her feet. The tall, dark man stood in the doorway, a smile of triumph on his lips. He closed the door softly behind him and said:

'Sit down, Tess. I haven't come to harm you or the old woman.'

The tall man walked across the small room, warmed his hands at the fire for a few minutes and then pulled one of the straight-backed wooden chairs to the far corner where he sat, only watching.

He had not come to harm her, he had said. Tess wondered, then why was he here? She thought she knew, and as she remained seated next to Mother Rose, a chill as deep as that which had fallen over the old woman entered her heart. She knew why he had come and there was nothing in the world she could do to stop it from happening.

When Ned Browning saw the thin wisps of smoke rising above the trees, he knew that his guess had been right. Tess and Mother Rose had chosen to hide in the line shack. But if they were hiding, why then start a fire to advertise their presence? He did not try to understand it without information to work with, he simply started the buckskin up along the winding trail toward the shack.

The prints of another horse were evident on the trail. Most of the trail was littered with pine needles, but here and there the dark earth was clear of debris, and there he could see clearly imprinted hoof prints even in this poor light. One rider. That was a puzzle. The horse was not the old gray, because Ned had seen the animal in the lean-to shelter at the Bright house.

Who, then?

A lone horse seemed to indicate that it was not a Colbert rider. Why would they have separated? It was puzzling, but again Ned Browning did not take the time to speculate when he had nothing but wild conjecture to work with. His sole concern was making sure that Tess and Mother Rose were safe.

That did not mean that he was not approaching the shack with caution. He had to assume that he was tracking an enemy, only because he had so few friends and he knew where most of them should be at this moment.

He should have suspected, might have known: pausing at the verge of the twilight-darkened timber he saw the paint horse standing before the tumble-down shack. It cocked its head curiously toward Ned. The man he had taken for the leader of the raiding party had seemed to be a cut above the rest of the rabble. A different sort of hunter. He had found Tess and he was waiting . . . waiting for. . . .

Who was he waiting for? It could not be Ned himself, since Ned was unknown to him and the gunman believed that Ned was well away from the mountain. For the return of Orson, Andy and the men? That could be, but then why choose to face them single-handedly?

Ned swung down from the buckskin horse, palmed his Colt and eased toward the door of the shack. Within, a low fire burned. The interior walls were painted with moving light and shadow. No one was speaking.

What now, then?

There was no good way to go about this. Ned merely stepped to the door, gun in hand and toed it open. He took in the situation with a glance. Tess sat in a wooden chair beside Mother Rose whose body was heaped with blankets, her face pale as ivory. Across the room sat the dark man Ned had met on the trail. The pistol in his hand was cocked and ready.

'Ned!' Tess said, rising to her feet.

'Don't move!' Santana ordered. To Ned he said: 'Who the hell are you?'

'Ned Browning. I told you before.'

'You told me a lot of things before,' Santana said, keeping his seat. The muzzle of his Colt was trained on Tess. 'What are you doing here?'

'I work for Orson Bright,' Ned said, his eyes flickering from Santana to the uncertain blue eyes of Tess. 'I lied to you on the trail because I wanted safe passage.'

'You just ran off and left these women behind?' Santana asked.

'I didn't know where they were,' Ned said honestly. 'When I found out they were missing I came back to find them.'

'Noble,' Santana said mockingly. He now shifted his feet and stood with catlike grace. Ned still held his own Colt, but he had no wish to start shooting in the confines of the tiny shack with two women present. He and Santana continued talking as if they were acquaintances who had not met for a while, catching up on events.

'What are *you* doing here?' Ned asked Santana.

'It's none of your business,' Santana said with a faint smile, 'but I am waiting for a man.' He tilted his head toward Tess, 'Her lover, Frank Lavender.'

Tess smiled and said: 'You'll have a long wait, Frank Lavender has never been my lover. He has never been on this mountain and never will be.'

'I guess you would say that,' Santana remarked. 'I heard otherwise. I've been hired to kill Lavender, and when I see him that is exactly what I'll do.'

Ned Browning was frowning deeply. He had

been told that *he* was Frank Lavender. The gunman did not seem to think so. 'You know him, do you?' Ned asked. 'Lavender, that is.'

'I know Frank. There was a time that we rode together. Though he was smarter then, it seems. The Frank Lavender I knew would not have risked getting tangled up in a fight like this for a—' his eyes shifted again to Tess. Ned was glad that Santana had not spoken whatever last word he had had in mind.

'What do we do now?' Ned asked.

'That's a question, isn't it? I don't want you hanging around, and I can't let you ride off to warn Frank. If I start shooting, it might bring other men on the run and that would warn Frank as well.' Santana shrugged. 'What do you suggest, drifter?'

'Just let us go,' Ned offered, not believing that Santana would. 'We won't talk.'

'Mother Rose can't be moved, Ned,' Tess said before Santana could respond. 'You could just leave, and—'

'I already said that he's not leaving,' Santana said sharply. He seated himself casually again. Ned, who had been thinking matters over, decided to tell the truth as he now knew it. Some of the truth.

'Listen to me. Frank Lavender is not here, he never has been here, as the lady told you. The rumor got started for some reason, I've heard it myself. But if Frank Lavender is here, he's a ghost. No one's ever seen him.'

'Ghosts don't participate in gunfights,' Santana said with quiet confidence. 'Everyone says that Lavender killed a gunhand named Royce Traylor in a shoot-out at a saloon in Hoyt's Camp.'

'Everyone is wrong,' Ned said. 'It had to have been someone impersonating Lavender.' *Who* it had been, he did not say, of course. At the same time Ned had been trying to assess his chances of shooting Santana without the women, one or both, being accidentally struck by bullets. The chances seemed slim, especially since Santana continued to keep his pistol barrel aimed in the direction of Tess as he had since Ned had entered the shack, believing that 'Frank Lavender' would not wish to see his woman shot.

Nor did Ned wish it.

'We have reached an impasse,' Santana said, 'have we not? I can't let you leave and yet I do not wish to kill you. I wonder if you could be convinced, if only for the sake of the women, to lay down your gun and sit quietly somewhere?'

At that moment Mother Rose groaned shallowly. Her legs twitched just enough to cause a ripple across the blankets covering her. Tess got to her knees beside the old woman's bed. She looked up at Ned with eyes that pleaded, but were filled with confusion.

'No,' Ned said with deliberation. 'I can't be convinced that it's in my best interests or that of the women to lay down my gun.'

'I thought not,' Santana said without obvious disappointment. He still held the upper hand and he knew it. 'I suppose it's up to me, then, to make some sort of decision.' Before the last word was out of his mouth, he had fired his pistol. Ned had been watching Santana closely, alert to any movement, or shift in manner. Even so, when it did happen, the shot was surprising, and surprisingly accurate.

Ned had seen the flicker of resolve in Santana's eyes and had thrown himself to one side as the bad man triggered off a round. The bullet slashed past Ned, ripping through his shirt, grooving its way through the flesh along his ribs. The night was filled briefly with blinding light and the sudden thunder of the gun.

Tess screamed as Santana leapt to his feet. Outside, against the cool earth, Ned continued to move. He managed to roll beneath Santana's startled paint horse without being stamped on, and he came up behind the outlaw's saddle, Colt cocked and ready. When Santana, back-lighted by the fire in the iron stove, appeared on the porch, Ned shot him dead.

Santana had been lifting his pistol at the same moment, but he had trouble finding Ned in the darkness. When Ned's bullet struck home, Santana's eyes went wide with disbelief. Perhaps, like many killers, Santana had never believed that he, too, could fall victim to the gun.

The outlaw fell to the ground and lay still in the night. Ned eased out from behind the horse, his legs trembling, his pistol still held at the ready in case Santana was not as dead as he appeared to be. Tess stood in the doorway, the fingertips of both hands touching her lips, her eyes reflecting shocked disbelief and relief at once. She started to rush toward Ned, stopped and waited as he walked unsteadily toward her.

Pausing to toe Santana's body and toss the gunman's pistol aside, Ned made his way to the door, holding his side.

'You're hurt,' Tess said. Ned shook his head negatively, although his side felt as if someone had laid a red-hot branding iron across it. The wound was bleeding, but not much. He was shaken, not from the impact of the bullet, but from knowing how near it had come to ending everything.

Mother Rose lay still on the cot, her face ashen. Ned did not think the old woman was breathing. 'I think the shock of the gunfire was too much on top of everything else,' Tess said in a faint voice. 'Her heart . . . she's gone, Ned.'

Ned had peeled off his shirt and Tess bound his side with a strip of cloth torn from Amos Shockley's not-so-clean sheet. There would be time later to clean the wound properly, not now. Now they had to go, and Ned knew it. The shot might bring more hunters. He told Tess to gather up whatever she owned.

'We can't go now!' she objected. 'Mother Rose . . . we can't just leave her here like that.'

'It has to be now, Tess,' Ned said sternly. 'We don't know who else is prowling around the forest. There could be more killers out there in the night.'

'But, Mother Rose—'

Ned interrupted her. 'Ask yourself if Mother Rose would rather see her dead husk buried or know that you got away safely. We go, Tess. Now!'

NINE

Outside they could now see the fires burning across the river, small red beacons in the darkness. 'They've torched Billy Lofton's house, Mack Paulsen's as well,' Ned said, answering Tess's unspoken question. 'It can't be long before someone will come to burn down your home as well. We have to get off the mountain.'

Ned swung into leather and told Tess to mount Santana's paint, but she refused. 'I can't,' she said nervously. 'A dead man's horse.'

'Swing up behind me then,' Ned said peevishly. Tess was willing to do that and he felt her arms around him, her cheek against his back. Taking the reins to Santana's horse he led the animal along behind them as they trailed back toward the Bright house.

'You'll have to ride the old gray horse,' Ned said as they wound their way through the timber. 'The buckskin has had some work today – I can't ask it to carry double all the way to Hoyt's Camp.'

'Is that where we're going? Hoyt's Camp?'

'Yes. You'll be safe there. Probably your father, Andy and all of the men are spending the night in town. The mule skinner wouldn't be willing to rent out his animals to tow the barges along a night road. There's too much risk of injuring one of them in the darkness.'

Tess was mounted on the hastily rigged gray horse as they finally started away from the house. The old animal seemed surprised to be moving, but was not balky. Deep in the shadows of the night forest, they still could see no glimmer of light from Hoyt's Camp. Ned said: 'Well, that dark-eyed killer made it pretty clear that I am not Frank Lavender, didn't he?'

'Yes,' Tess replied.

'Then why did your father tell me that story about his having hired me?'

'He needed help, Ned. He was desperate for any help at all.'

Ned could understand it, but that did not mean he appreciated having been put in this

134

dangerous situation. After another half mile, he spoke again: 'Who am I then, Tess?'

'I don't know, Ned. If I did I would tell you, but the truth is no one knows.'

'Hell of a way to go through life,' he muttered without looking at the blond girl riding beside him.

Eventually they emerged on the hilltop overlooking Hoyt's Camp. At a distance it was silent and small, the glow of its many lamps barely illuminating the patch of prairie where it stood. 'You go directly to the hotel,' Ned instructed Tess. 'You can ask at the desk if anyone you know is registered there. If not . . . stay there anyway. Don't take it upon yourself to ride back to the ranch no matter what.'

His words were stern, his face set. Tess, who had no intention of trying to return to the ranch, did not understand his dark mood. She did, however, know him well enough to see that there was something else on Ned Browning's mind.

'What is it, Ned? What are you going to do?'

'Keep Frank Lavender alive for just a little longer,' Ned answered.

'I don't understand you.'

'Tess, a man was sent to kill me. And if

135

someone had been around to identify me as Frank Lavender, or rather the man using Lavender's name, Santana would have done the job without mercy. He was sent, as I say. That is, he was hired by someone and there is only one man who could have done that.'

'Lyle Colbert?'

Ned nodded. 'I intend to pay him a little visit. Maybe Ned Browning couldn't arrange a meeting with Colbert, but I guarantee you he will talk to Frank Lavender.' He paused. 'Especially now that his hired executioner is dead.'

'You'll get yourself killed, Ned! It's a crazy idea.'

'Maybe. What do I care, really? I am a nameless, homeless man who is probably an outlaw on the run. I have a chance to do something – for all of you. Right now, the houses that Billy Lofton and Mack Paulsen worked to build are burning, and probably your house will be next. What gives Colbert his sense of power? No man owns a river, and throwing a chain across it does not make it so. He has to be run out of the territory once and for all to keep this from continuing.'

'You make it sound noble,' Tess said with some heat. 'It's not! It's just suicidal.'

'It doesn't matter much,' he shrugged. 'No one can miss a man who doesn't even exist.' They had reached the outskirts of Hoyt's Camp. The settlement, so silent at a distance, revealed itself now as a boisterous, rollicking timber town.

'Remember what I said,' Ned told Tess. 'Go directly to the hotel – and stay there!'

'Ned,' Tess said as he turned his horse's head southward, toward Lyle Colbert's stronghold, 'you are wrong. You do exist, and *I* would miss you very much if something were to happen to you.'

The road leading south, toward Lyle Colbert's house, passed through rolling hills. Here only scattered pines grew, most of the former timberland having been cleared during the construction of Hoyt's Camp. There was a low crescent moon rising slowly in the east as if it were an effort to crest the mountains. The buckskin, although weary, moved easily beneath Ned Browning. There seemed to be few men around. Some of the Colbert gang had crossed the river to destroy the property of Billy Lofton and Mack Paulsen, others may have been dispatched to the sawmill or into Hoyt's Camp to confront the timbermen. Ned did not try to guess Lyle Colbert's plan. He was in sight of the long house, before he was even approached.

'Alvin, is that you? someone called from out of the darkness. Then: 'Hey you, who are you, and where do you think you're going?'

Ned reined in and sat his saddle loosely, hands on the pommel. Two riders appeared out of the night shadows and squinted at Ned. Both had rifles across their saddlebows. 'What do you want?' one of the men asked.

'I need to see Lyle Colbert,' Ned said easily.

'Oh, you do? And just who in hell are you?'

'My name's Frank Lavender,' Ned replied smoothly. The two guards stiffened. One of them walked his horse forward a few steps, peering at Ned.

'It is Lavender!' the man, the one who had been with Royce Traylor when Ned shot him said. 'I know him from the saloon.'

'Lavender,' the other, older man said hesitantly. 'What are you doing here?'

'I already told you. I need to talk to Lyle Colbert.'

'Did you know that Santana's after you?' the younger man asked.

'No,' Ned said, 'he's not. Not anymore.'

'You don't mean. . . ? But you and Santana used to ride together, didn't you?'

'A long time ago,' Ned answered. 'Anyway, he came looking for me. I did what I had to do – business is business. That's the reason I want to talk to Colbert. Business is business, and he's down a man now.' *Santana.* So that was who the dark man had been. Ned remembered that Santana was the one who had murdered the elder Bright son, Dan. Well, that was one old debt repaid.

'I don't know if we should let you through,' Ned was told.

Ned's answering smile was visible in the faint light of the coming moon. 'Boys,' he said coldly, 'I don't think you can keep me from it.'

The younger man, the one he had sized up as reluctant to fight back in the saloon, turned his eyes away. The other Colbert rider was thoughtful.

'I suppose maybe we couldn't, Lavender. But do you mind if we just ride along with you?'

'Grateful for the company,' Ned said, and he started the buckskin forward, the two Colbert men trailing him, muttering to each other.

Another few minutes found them in the yard of the Colbert house and Ned swung down, loosely tying his horse to the wrought iron-supported hitch rail there.

'You two coming in?' he asked affably.

'We'll see you to the door,' the older rider said. 'Just to make sure.'

Ned shrugged, stepped up onto the awning-covered front porch and rapped at the door. 'You don't need to do that,' he was advised. 'Just go on in.'

Ned palmed the doorknob and stepped into a carpeted entranceway decorated with antlers and a striped Indian blanket. The two Colbert men followed at a safe distance, their rifles held waist-high.

'Let me ask the boss first,' one of the guards said. 'Charlie, you know what to do if he starts anything.' Then the guard tramped down a short corridor to a heavy oaken door where he rapped and entered. After a minute he returned. There was a look of surprise on his face.

'He says he'll see you.'

'Fine,' Ned replied.

'He says he'll see you if you aren't wearing a gun.'

Ned shrugged and shucked his Colt, handing it grips-first to the older man. 'Don't lose it,' he said. No one smiled in return. Taking a deep slow breath, Ned walked down the corridor to the now-open oaken door and entered.

Lyle Colbert sat behind his desk, wearing a dark-blue town suit, starched white shirt and black bolo tie. The clawlike fingers of his right hand were resting on an ivory-handled Colt .44. A fire burned low in a native-stone fireplace, casting spirit shadows on the wall. Behind Colbert's desk was a tall window flanked by red velvet drapes. Beyond the window Ned could see the moon lifting itself higher into the sky.

Colbert's sapphire eyes glittered as he studied Ned Browning. 'What do you want?' he demanded, stroking the pistol resting on his desk. 'Is it true that you killed Santana?'

'It's true. As to what I want, Colbert, I want work. No, it's not the work. I want money. As much as I can milk the situation for.'

Colbert relaxed mentally just a little. The motivation was one he could understand. 'What about your loyalty to—'

'Loyalty don't fill the purse,' Ned snapped. 'I kind of like that little girl of Bright's, and I thought I'd give him a hand. But I saw what I was up against soon enough, and I don't like hanging my life out on a limb for nothing. The loggers promised me money, it turns out they don't really have any. At least not enough.'

'You are usually well paid, I take it,' Colbert said in his thin voice.

'I command more than Santana ever did,' Ned answered. 'You shouldn't have to ask why. Look who's standing here now.'

'Yes, I see.' Colbert's eyes narrowed. 'I wonder if I could trust you, Lavender. You were working for the loggers. Now you claim that you want to change sides. I can't say much for Santana, but he was loyal. When he hired on to do a job, it was always done, without second thoughts.'

Colbert's long-nailed hand tightened around the ivory grips of the Colt revolver. 'No, Lavender. I just don't think I can afford you.'

The pistol came up and fired. Colbert wasn't much of a shot. The bullet whined past Ned as he dove for the floor and rolled away from the desk. When he came to his feet he found himself beside the fireplace, and as Colbert fired again, another wildly aimed shot which sang off the stone hearth, Ned grabbed the end of a burning

142

brand and flung it at Colbert.

Colbert fell to the side of his chair, trying to dodge the burning log and Ned moved. He leaped on top of Colbert's desk and, not pausing to look at Colbert, flung himself against the window, leading with his shoulder. He hit the dark earth outside, rising in a bed of shards. Ducking low, keeping below the window, he raced in a crouch for the corner of the house where he stood, taking in deep gulps of cold night air.

Colbert had not fired again, and now smoke was billowing from the window. The velvet drapes had caught fire and gone up quickly. Ned hesitated, watching the creeping flames. Was Colbert still in there, out cold after his fall, or had he made it to the door and down the corridor? He would not leave the man to burn to death, no matter what. He began making his way back toward the shattered window.

'Hold it right there!' a triumphant voice behind Ned called out.

Raising his hands, Ned turned to see the red-faced, jug-eared man he had met on the mountain. The one who had wanted to kill him there. He recalled the man's name.

'Jeter!'

'I knew you were trouble from the start. You fooled Santana, but not me,' Jeter said, stepping nearer, his pistol leveled.

'Jeter, I think Colbert's still in there,' Ned said, nodding toward the fire which now could be heard crackling and growling as it made its way up the plank walls toward the ceiling. 'We have to find out.'

Jeter didn't laugh, but his smile was a scornful expression. 'That's a clever try, mister. 'I don't think we should go back there. I think you ought to precede me into the yard. Or,' Jeter shrugged, 'I can just kill you here. It makes no difference to me.'

Ned Browning tried pleading again, but got nowhere. Either Jeter's loyalty was thin or he placed more importance on capturing one of the enemy to display to the other men. Ned believed that he could now smell flesh burning, but he hoped not. He would have had no compunctions about shooting Lyle Colbert in a fight, but to die that way. . . .

'Are you going to move or am I going to kill you where you stand!' Jeter shrieked.

What choice did he have? Keeping his hands held high, Ned turned his back on the burning room and started toward the front of the house.

It was chaos there.

Two men were fleeing the fire which had already started burning among the rafters while others rushed toward the blaze with a futile array of fire buckets. Among these were the two men who had acted as Ned's guards. Horses whickered wildly and reared. Breaking free of their tethers, these made a dash for safety while their riders tried to chase them down. The flames were streaking the sky. Golden sparks shot high and floating ash sifted down. Jeter found his moment of triumph stolen from him. No one paid any attention to him and his captured enemy.

Seizing the opportunity, Ned stepped away from Jeter a few strides, grabbed a man by the arm and shouted: 'Did Colbert get out?'

'Not that I saw. No one's been able to get in that far. Maybe he made it through the side window.'

He hadn't. Ned knew that for a fact.

A man straining with the weight of the two water buckets he carried approached Ned on the smoke-shadowed porch. With a glance at the momentarily baffled Jeter, Ned said, 'Let me have one of those,' and took a bucket. Entering the

145

house with two other men, Ned could see that the battle against the raging fire was a lost cause.

'We can't do anything else but watch it burn,' he said. No one asked him who he was or what he was doing there. The fire made all other thoughts inconsequential. 'We'd better just pull back ourselves!' he shouted 'Some of the trees will catch, and we don't want to be standing near them when it happens.'

'Let's get our ponies out of the stable!' a big-shouldered man suggested. Ned stayed close beside him as they exited the house, scarves held to their faces, black smoke rolling past them, hot flame at their heels.

Jeter was only briefly confused. He was able to pick Ned out of the retreating band of men, but what was he to do? Start firing into the crowd? He hurried after the smoke-streaked band of outlaws.

Someone had already opened the gate to the corral, and those horses had scattered widely into the fire-brightened night, but the stable itself still held half a dozen horses, rearing and complaining in their stalls as the scent of fire and smoke grew stronger. The Colbert men unlatched the stall doors and grabbed for their own horses, some not bothering to collect their tack.

146

No one had claimed the big sorrel Ned found quivering in the rear stall and so he swung the gate wide and mounted the horse bareback, heeling it roughly to urge it into a running start. Jeter again was not fooled.

The outlaw stood near the stable doors and when Ned rode the sorrel down on him, he stepped nimbly aside and fired his Colt three times. The second bullet caught Ned in the shoulder, and he reeled in the saddle.

Clinging to the horse's mane, he ran the sorrel as far as it could continue the frantic pace. The sky went from fire-bright to pitch black as Ned rode the horse into the sheltering forest toward the river. He was having difficulty holding on now. His vision blurred and his shoulder was shot through with pain.

He rode until he could keep his grip no more. Then he slowed the horse which was breathing hard, trembling now. His dismount was a sagging headfirst slide to the cold earth. The sorrel sidestepped away from its human burden and Ned lay still for a long minute, his shoulder fiery and throbbing.

The sound of a horse approaching brought him to his feet, his body responding reluctantly.

Still he made it up, and he was ready and braced when Jeter burst from the trees, his rifle at the ready, his eyes bright with a killing fury.

TEN

The first shot from Jeter's Winchester flared in the night, yellow-red and horrible in its intent. But the man was over-eager, and he had fired before his pony had fully halted. The bullet flew past Ned's head, doing no damage. It was the muzzle flash that had an effect. His eyes, already blurred with pain seemed to have gone blind with the flash of brilliant light.

He took to his heels. Weaving wildly through the forest he ran on through the night, unarmed hurting and desperate. He had no doubt that Jeter was behind him. The man was determined to see Ned Browning dead.

Ahead something gleamed. There was a low murmuring which grew louder until it became a rushing sound, and Ned realized that he was looking at the river flowing swiftly past. He stopped, chest filled with fiery pain, legs wobbling. He could not see Jeter, but he knew he was behind him somewhere. Jeter must have known that he now had Ned pinned against the river and that there was nowhere left to run. He was taking his time approaching, but he would come, confident and quite deadly. Ned stumbled on until he stood at the very edge of the swift-flowing Snake River. He paused again. He could not go on. Could not!

Jeter appeared wraithlike from the dark forest, and he raised his rifle to his shoulder. Somehow he missed his shot again, but Ned did not wait for a second shot. He threw himself into the icy river and let it sweep him away. Jeter did not fire again. Perhaps he thought that he had tagged Ned with his first bullet.

It made no difference. Within minutes Ned was swept far downstream, the current surging around him. He had saved his skin by diving into the river, but now what? The current was far too strong for him to swim. The forest bunched close against the shore, tall sentinel silhouettes in serrated ranks. And he was drifting farther from them, bullied along his way by the relentless current.

It was a struggle just to stay above water with his injured shoulder. He could only watch the ranks of trees rushing past, the river surging on. His strength was rapidly fading. Twice his head went under and twice he rose sputtering and spitting out cold water. He did not think he could survive a third plunge into the icy river. The stars, he saw, were bright, silver, far-flung in a black sky. The moon was a pale mocking eye in the east. They symbolized nothing to him. Dead orbs. He was ready to join them in their dead realm, to give it up. What was the point in struggling against the inevitable?

His body was thrown harshly against an unseen obstruction, driving the wind from his tortured chest. His movement was stopped dead although the current ripped by and clawed at his body. A rock? An unseen snag? He probed for the object with his hand. It seemed to be firmly fixed, and yet it was swaying. Cold, serpentlike. . . .

The chain! He had come up against the anchored north shore end of the massive chain. He was fifty feet or so from the riverbank, he saw. If he could only drag himself shoreward. He began to inch his way toward land. His right shoulder had no usable strength in it and so he simply gripped with that hand and pulled himself forward with his still-sore left arm. The current slapped against him, shifting even the monstrous weight of the chain as the river swept past.

It was no use. He knew that after another ten minutes, fifteen. He was never going to make it to the beach. The distance was impossible. He was frozen to the bone. His body was slow to respond to his commands or failed to respond at all. His lungs burned, his vision was blurred and the river rushed on, powerful, inexorable. His strength was waning, dying.

He could not make it. The night went black, colder, fading to nothingness.

The nightmare had returned to haunt him. The men without faces, wearing badges, stood silently around him. This time he was lying down instead of standing among them. One of the shadowy figures bent low over him and a voice that sounded as if it were coming from the depths of a well said, 'Hello, Walt. Welcome back.'

Ray? Ray Holden?

'Ray?'

'It's me, Walt,' the lawman said. 'We didn't think you were going to make it for a while.

Welcome back to the land of the living.'

Slowly, as his vision cleared, he recognized the other two deputy marshals, George Shaftner and Willie Randall. They both stood smiling down at him, hats held in their hands.

'Where was I? Where am I . . . how?'

'Take it easy,' Holden said. 'You're in a hotel room in Hoyt's Camp. They were towing the timber barges upriver this morning when they came upon you lying on the beach. They brought you into town – a man named Bright and a couple of others whose names I didn't get.'

'Orson Bright?'

'That's it. Do you remember him, Walt?'

'Like someone out of a dream,' was the reply.

'Bright seemed to know you well enough, but he didn't seem to know your name.'

'No . . . no, but then neither did I. Can you fill me in a little, Ray? My memory seems to have some holes in it.'

'We sent you up here from Cheyenne to look into the timber wars. It seems that you took care of that all right! They tell us Lyle Colbert is dead and his men scattered. To top that, you got that renegade Santana as well. You'll have to tell us all about it when you're feeling better.'

153

'I don't know if I recall it all. What happened to me in the first place, Ray? On the road to Hoyt's Camp, I mean.'

'The Liggett boys and a couple of their friends. You recall Dave and Lawrence Liggett? You got them for rustling about a year ago. They came back to settle accounts. When they found out that you were riding out alone, they decided to ambush you.'

'The Liggetts—' They, too, seemed only a hazy memory.

'George, Willie and I went out looking for you when you didn't wire us from Hoyt's Camp. We found your horse . . . dead . . . and Willie tracked you to the edge of the Snake River Gorge. We figured you for dead. No man could take that fall and survive. I guess we underestimated you again. Good work, Walt. I suppose we'd better let you get your rest now.'

Dusk had settled over the town when he awakened again. There were other people in his room now, three of them. With difficulty he recognized Orson Bright, Andy and the girl he had thought he had known only his dreams.

'Tess!'

154

'It's me,' she said. Concern shaded her eyes, but she managed a brave little smile. Orson Bright eased up to the foot of the bed, Andy at his shoulder.

'Good to see you alive, son,' Orson said. 'We didn't think you'd make it. Was it you that burned down Lyle Colbert's house?'

'I don't know,' he answered honestly. 'I was there.'

'No matter. The rascal is dead. His gang is scattered. I don't think they'll be back.'

'No, men like that don't fight for no wages.'

'They told you about Santana, didn't they?' Andy said excitedly. 'I found him when I went looking for Tess and Mother Rose. Do you remember getting him? That was a long time coming. The man who killed my brother, Dan. Did you know that the girl, Doris Hancock, came back to town and she's telling everyone now that it wasn't a fair fight that got Dan. Santana cut him down from an alleyway.'

'You're babbling on,' Orson Bright growled. 'Can't you see the man's still tired. There is one thing I'd like to say,' Orson said. 'I'm sorry I lied to you. In the end, though, you did earn the money I promised. You got rid of Colbert and

Santana. I've two hundred dollars now, after the sale of my timber. I'd like to offer it to you.'

'No,' the man on the bed replied firmly. 'I'm a lawman, and you know a lawman can't accept money for doing his job. I'm sure you have better uses for it, anyway.'

'Well, thank you, Mr . . . Marshal—?'

'Walt Strahan,' the wounded man said with a twisted smile. 'It sounds odd to *me* now, but that's my name'

'Well, then, Marshal Strahan, I guess we'll be going. That's about all we came to say.'

'I haven't had my say,' Tess said. She looked at her father, at Andy.

'Well, say it,' Orson prompted. Andy nudged his father in the ribs and Orson's expression changed. 'Oh,' he said, and together he and Andy eased out of the room.

Tess pulled a chair up to the bedside and cocked her head. 'Do you make a habit of doing this?' she asked. 'Getting shot up, I mean?'

'You might not believe it, but I've only been wounded twice in the line of duty. And each time I've awakened to find you at my bedside.'

'Does that mean that I'm bad luck?' Tess asked.

'Bad . . . I was just thinking how lucky I've been

to have you there when I needed someone.'

'Do you plan on continuing in law enforcement?'

'I don't know, Tess, I haven't had the time to think about it.'

'Well, I don't suppose it matters one way or the other. We'll find a way to get along.'

'We'll . . . Tess, what are you saying?'

She had taken his hand between her own and now her smile deepened. 'I'm proposing to you, of course! If I wait for you to say anything, I'll be an old woman and still waiting.'

'Oh.'

' "Oh". That's your answer?'

'It's a kind of new thought. Why don't you let me have a small kiss while I think about it?'

Tess bent low and kissed him and when she withdrew he was grinning. 'I guess you'll do all right,' he teased.

'Well, that's settled then,' Tess said. 'It wasn't very romantic, but it's settled. There's just one thing, Mr Whatever.'

'Walter Strahan.'

'Mr Strahan. It's a good enough name. Yes, I can carry that name. If I call you 'Ned' now and then, just let it go.'

157

'I'm pleased,' Walt Strahan said with a straight face, 'that my name is good enough for you.'

'Good! It's better than good, Walt. Imagine going through life as Mrs Hezekiah Pybomoski!'

Walt pondered that odd comment as sundown blanketed the town of Hoyt's Camp with soft darkness. He would ask her sometime what she had meant. Right now it seemed quite unimportant. She was holding his hand still, and as his eyes closed again, the settling night spread its healing peace over his bed.

When the hotel room door slowly opened, the hinges creaked slightly, and Walt Strahan, who had been half-awake anyway due to the pain in his shoulder, came instantly alert. He thought he recognized the figure silhouetted in the doorway, but was not sure until he spoke.

'This is the end of the line,' Jeter said, thumbing back the hammer of his Colt revolver.

Walt Strahan threw himself from the bed. He landed on the wooden floor with a jolt that shot fresh pain through his body but he caused Jeter to miss his shot. Little good it would do him. As he tried to sit up, to stand, Jeter took three steps toward him, cocking his weapon again.

Walt saw the second shadowy figure in the

doorway, heard a muffled curse. Jeter spun at the sound of footsteps and tried to fire at the shadow, but Andy Bright's shot was quicker and truer.

'Heard someone in the hall passing my room. He had his gun out. Knew whoever it was he was up to no good,' Andy said in a shaky voice. No matter his eagerness to be a fighting man, this was the first time Andy Bright had ever taken a life, and it was obvious that the young man didn't like the feeling.

Other feet were rushing toward the room. Walt had lifted himself to sit on the bed. Andy had touched fire to the bedside lamp's wick.

'Everything all right?' Ray Holden asked loudly. He had his pistol drawn as did George Shaftner. Both lawmen eased into the room, looking down at the still form of Jeter. On their heels Tess rushed in, still in her night dress, wrapper thrown loosely around her shoulders. Holden had crouched to examine the dead man.

'Who was he, Walt?' the marshal saked.

'The last shadow of Frank Lavender,' Walt said. Glancing at Tess, he added, 'And the last echo of Ned Browning.'